FATAL FLOSS

STITCHES IN CRIME
BOOK 8

ACF BOOKENS

1

I tightened the last bolt on our solar chicken door and sat back to look at my work. It was a little crooked and I could see daylight on one side, but it worked. It would keep out predators. "Good enough for a Sutton," I said to my four-year-old son Sawyer next to me. "Want to try it out?"

Given Sawyer's level of excitement, I might have just asked him if he wanted to get a puppy, which I was definitely *not* asking. Fifteen new chicks were enough tiny animals for this single mom.

Saw jumped up and slapped his still-chubby fingers over the solar gauge, then pumped his fist in the air when the door slid shut. "We did it!" he shouted. "You are a genius, Mom."

I smiled. I'd started saying that when I successfully constructed his wooden train set without any extraneous pieces, and he'd quickly picked up on the saying ... Not that I discouraged him.

"We are both geniuses," I said. "We make a good team." I put my hand out for him to give me a high five. "Now, are you ready to go get our chicks?"

It was early September, and I'd let Sawyer stay home from

preschool today just so that we could go to the post office together to pick up our new baby birds. I'd ordered chicks from a hatchery and received them in the mail several times, but it never failed to amaze me that living creatures were shipped like dog treats. Even so, the chicks from this hatchery were almost always quite healthy and quite loud when they arrived.

That loudness was the reason Saw and I got up extra early and got the coop door installed. We wanted to be able to go get the birds as soon as we got the call from the post office, and that call had come in ten minutes ago. I didn't want to make the postal workers have to put up with fifteen tiny peeping voices for any longer than necessary.

"Yes," Sawyer said and bolted for the car. Then, he paused and looked back, shouting, "We're not taking Beauregard, right?"

I shook my head vigorously. Definitely not. Our Maine Coon cat, Beau, was typically very laid back, if slightly crotchety, but even his apathy and laziness might be disrupted by the sight of day-old chicks. "No, baby birds and kitties don't mix," I said.

It was going to be a chicken-filled day. After we brought our babies back and installed them in the brooder we'd made from a tote, we were going over to our neighbor Jackie's house to take down her old chicken coop. She'd never used it, and lately raccoons had been taking up residence in the building. I had told her that I could probably use the wood in my architectural salvage business, and she'd offered to give it to me if I took down the building. I was happy to trade labor for product most days, but especially when it was a kindness for a neighbor.

Given that the building was pretty small, I thought Sawyer and I could probably handle it by ourselves. And I'd told Saw that he could have some of the wood to build something of his own to sell in the shop. The boy was surprisingly good with a hammer, and even if whatever he made came out really wonky,

I knew two grandparents who would proudly make the purchase for their own home.

The chicks were as loud as expected when we got to the post office, and Sawyer spent the whole ride back to our house talking to them and imitating their peeps at ever louder volume. By the time we got them out of the box, dipped their beaks into the water to teach them to drink, introduced them to the food, and checked the temperature under the heat lamp, I was ready for the alternative noise of hammers and crowbars.

We walked over to Jackie's house, and as we strolled down her long drive, I looked at the small white house that sat facing the back of mine on the small hill across the ravine created by the train tracks. On the historic map of the area, that white house was here early, as early as 1838, and I enjoyed looking at it and thinking about the farmer that had lived there. Maybe a bachelor. Maybe a young couple.

They had likely farmed most of the land around us for subsistence and a small profit. And while I imagined the chicken coop we were about to take down had at least been re-sided if not entirely rebuilt in the centuries since the farm was established, it probably sat on the same spot as every coop before it. Geographic change was not something that came easily on farm spaces.

We walked up onto Jackie's porch, me via the steps and Sawyer via her wheelchair ramp, and before he could even ring the doorbell, she was there with her taupe glasses and warm smile. "Hi, Saw," she shouted. "Would you rather walk in or get a wheelie ride?"

Saw looked at her and said, "Wheelie, please!" before climbing into her lap in her wheelchair and letting her spin him around and then give him a wheelie ride into the living room.

Jackie had used a wheelchair her whole life, and she was a master with that thing. While it had taken Saw a while to realize that Jackie could just let him take it for a ride after she shifted to the recliner she used for work, he was always glad to get a ride from her when she offered, which was pretty much every time we came over.

His ride over, Saw settled into the couch and helped himself to the small bowl of Hershey's Kisses that Jackie kept on her side table. The boy really knew how to make himself at home. While I wanted to scold him, I also knew Jackie didn't mind. She and Sawyer had become fast friends in the past few months, and now she was his favorite babysitter ... partially because she was really fun but also because she always had chocolate.

"We're ready to work," Sawyer said around a mouthful of chocolate.

I rolled my eyes. "Don't talk with your mouth full," I said. "Hi, Jackie. How are you?"

"I'm good. Thanks for doing this, Paisley. I love raccoons from afar, but those suckers are a real nuisance when they take up residence." Apparently, a mother raccoon had given birth to a litter of adorable masked babies a couple of weeks back, and they had been littering Jackie's backyard with garbage that they brought in from who knows where. She shook her head. "It's like having a bunch of short, masked frat boys living out back."

"I bet. Just the squirrels nesting in our oak out front are loud enough to startle me sometimes. I can't imagine a family of raccoons," I said with a laugh.

"Do we get to see the raccoons?" Sawyer said

My heart stopped. I had not thought of this possibility. I could have kicked myself.

Jackie glanced at my face and then cracked up. "Don't worry, Paisley. Animal Control came earlier in the week and relocated them. It's just the building left."

The rhythm of my heart picked up again. "Oh good. That makes things easier."

Saw was of a different mind, and I thought we might have a bit of a meltdown on our hands. But I handed him the small hammer and crowbar my dad had gotten for him, and he immediately forgot about the raccoons in favor of destruction. "Let's go, Mom!"

I waved to Jackie as we went outside and around to the back of her beautiful farmhouse. This one had been built in the early part of the nineteenth century and featured the standard kitchen and living room of an old farmhouse with two bedrooms upstairs, but Jackie had put on a large addition at the back with a master bedroom, luxurious bathroom, and a closet the size of my first floor.

She'd made her money in banking, and while she was retired now, she still covered her expenses and more with her wise investment strategy. Every year, she took a month-long vacation to a country she hadn't yet visited, and I looked forward to seeing her photos on social media so I could live vicariously through her experiences. This year, she'd gone to Iceland, and after seeing her photos I was so jealous that I promised myself that Saw and I could go there in the next couple of years.

The coop was long and low, with horizontal boards spanning the length. The wood itself had a lovely gray patina, and as long as we got most of the boards off intact, they could make nice flooring for a small space. Of course, the trick here was going to be preventing Sawyer from causing mass destruction.

I had explained to him that we were going to sell these boards and we needed to have them intact, and he had seemed to understand that. But as soon as we got to the coop, he slung the hammer back like he was going to pound the first board into pieces. It was then that I decided Sawyer needed his first lesson in capitalism.

"Saw, if you help me get these boards off without breaking

them, I'll give you some of the money from selling them." This got his attention, and he stopped mid-swing.

He turned to me and, with all the seriousness of a child who is going to be a fierce negotiator, said, "I want two fives."

I feigned that I was considering his offer and said, "Okay. If you help me get the boards off without breaking them, I will give you two fives. And if you're really good and listen carefully, I will give you three fives. That's fifteen dollars."

A giant smile broke across his face. "Okay, Mama." He turned the hammer in his hand like a pro and began gently pulling on the board with the claw. I guess all that work hammering and removing nails with his grandfather was paying off, and a little bribery didn't hurt either.

For the next hour, Sawyer and I worked diligently, and I was stunned by his focus for so long. But eventually, his attention started to wander, and I kept an ear out for him as he trotted around the yard gathering flowers and following butterflies. Eventually he settled down to dig a hole in an old flower bed behind the coop. Since he was using a stick, the going was slow, and I had enough time to get the rest of the boards off before I could tell he was done with manual labor for the day. Fortunately, I'd planned ahead and timed things well, it seemed.

"All right, Love Bug," I said when I heard tires on the gravel driveway. "Boppy is here to take you for ice cream and to visit the playground. I'll see you at home in a little while."

Sawyer leaped up with delight when he saw not just his grandfather but his grandmother, too, coming around the corner of the house. My boy loved my dad, but he had a special affection for Lucille. The idea that both of them would be taking him to the playground and pushing him on swings and playing monster chase – well, it was a four-year-old's delight.

I waved as they intercepted him and took his hands to swing-walk him to the car. We had all learned that when Saw moved quickly from one place to another, it was best to go with the flow and not try to slow down for things like greeting, cordiality, or small talk. Dad and Lucille were coming over for dinner, so I'd catch up with them later.

Now, I could get to the hard work on the coop: the work that I didn't want to share with a small child who could not keep from touching things, including chicken excrement. It was helpful that we were down to the stud walls now, providing extra ventilation, but it was still going to be a dusty, dirty job of clearing the floorboards to see if we could salvage them to clean and sand. I wasn't looking forward to it.

But this project was a job for a friend, and it would yield some good boards for someone to reuse. I slipped on my respirator and headed in. Fortunately, the coop had been kept relatively clean over the years, but no matter how tidy a coop is, chickens are dirty animals and even the best bird keepers can't clean up all of the poop, all of the time.

I began by sweeping out as much as I could of the dust and other deposits off the floor and onto the tarps I'd laid around the building. My plan was to gather up the tarps and drag them to the woods to let the dust be part of the natural ecosystem. It quickly became clear, however, that the dust was going to become a part of the lawn since the wind had picked up and begun creating a cloud around the building.

"Did someone set off a smoke bomb?" I heard a familiar voice say.

When I saw Santiago, my fiancé, step through the dust with his own respirator on, I laughed. "Looks like it, doesn't it? But nope, it's just dust mites and poop."

"Oh, much better," he said. "How can I help?"

I smiled at him. "I didn't expect you here today. I thought you were on duty."

"I was, but the new guy came in, so I begged off." The edges of his eyes crinkled, which told me he was smiling. "I couldn't pass up the chance to see my fiancée in this particular glory."

A blush rose up under my skin, and I grinned behind my own breathing device. We had only been engaged a few months, but it had been an amazing and busy few months. We had plans to marry in April, and we wanted to do as much of the event ourselves at my farmhouse as we could. Even with the informal theme and our house as the venue, we still had to book a lot of things as soon as possible. Lucille was doing our cake, and she and our friend Mary Johnson were going to handle the catering, too. Yet, Santi and I were still trying to decide on flavors and menu items. Plus, we had decor to choose and our attendants to select. Music, favors, tent, chairs, tables – it all got so overwhelming when I started to think through things.

So mostly, I didn't. Santiago and I had agreed to set aside two hours a weekend to power through as much planning as we could, and then the rest would have to wait until the next weekend. Given how busy we both were, this solution was working, even if it left me a little breathless with anxiety in between.

Now, though, I was glad to see him for something other than flipping through wedding magazines and talking about the costs and the pros & cons of serving alcohol. He took to the work with great fervor, and before I knew it, the floorboards were up, the rafters lifted, and the entire structure picked apart into two piles – "keep" and "burn." I was happy to see that the *keep* pile was quite substantial and included a lot of the floorboards, which were thick oak and could be used for the same purpose when cleaned.

The fun part came now, when we got to burn the detritus. I texted Jackie to let her know we were getting started, and a few moments later, she came out with a tray of s'mores makings on her lap. "I know, I know. We can't cook marshmallows over chicken dookie, but I had the kid who does my yard set up a fire in the pit for after we light this one." She pointed back behind her toward the house. "You can't have a bonfire, even with poop, without marshmallows. It's a rule."

I laughed. "I like your rules," I said as I tucked some loose newspapers under the pile of trash wood that Santi had just built. He threw on some lighter fluid, probably more than was necessary, and tossed in a match. The flame shot up like a reverse rocket engine, and I was a little sad that Sawyer couldn't see it. But my sadness was matched by relief that I didn't have to keep him from seeing how fast various sticks would burn in that heat.

Jackie led us over to the actual firepit, and without lighter fluid this time, Santi lit a second pile of newspaper and sticks. The three of us sat around roasting marshmallows and eating s'mores while we chatted about the big news in town: the decision that the county board of supervisors had made to not allow any more franchised businesses to build within county limits. All of us were pleased by the decision, even though we realized it might mean fewer jobs for some folks, but as small business owners, Jackie and I both appreciated both this decision and the tax incentives the county had put in for local folks to start their own companies.

"Going to be a big help to me," Jackie said. "It's hard to run a virtual assisting business when I'm paying taxes through the nose. Those breaks will help me do more than just break even."

"Yep, me, too. And Mika's store will see a big boost. I know the retailers in town have a hard time justifying their storefronts with the slim foot traffic on Main Street. This should help." My best friend Mika's yarn store was very popular with the local knitters and crocheters, and she had built a good following online and at the Charlottesville market, too. But yarn is not a necessity, and in a place like Octonia, where a lot of folks live below the poverty line, she was barely surviving some months.

I stood up and brushed off my hands. "Only one thing left

to do," I said as I walked back toward the square of bare earth where the coop had stood. "My favorite part."

Santiago shook his head. "I've never met a woman who likes to play in dirt as much as you do," he laughed. "She gets such a thrill out of finding trash," he said to Jackie.

"Not me," Jackie said as she moved toward the house. "I'll leave you to it, but if you find gold doubloons, you know where to find me."

I smiled and waved as I headed back to grab my rake and begin the hunt for anything that had been thrown or fallen under the coop. I didn't expect gold coins, but maybe a button or a cool old bottle or two. I had just been reading *The Last Apothecary*, so I imagined myself as Caroline Parcewell mudlarking in the Thames as I began to gently rake back the piles that had accumulated under the coop.

It took me a few minutes to get past the first layer of old poop, but then, I started turning up the good stuff – a small blue jar with a glass eyedropper in it, a piece of green glass as thick as my thumb, and even a wheat penny that Sawyer would love to add to his collection, once I washed it.

I was just getting down into the dirt when my leaf rake skimmed over something much more firmly stuck in the ground. I raked away as much as I could from the yellowish edge I could see peeking out of the ground and tried to temper my imagination's whims of colonoware pots or some fine Royal Doulton jug. As I bent down to use my fingers to free the item from the soil, I pictured myself on *Antiques Roadshow,* my jaw sagging as a British woman with a stylish brooch told me that my find was one of the finest pieces of ceramic she'd ever seen.

I had visions of putting away enough money from the sale of the delicate platter – my visions were getting grander as I dug – for Sawyer to attend undergrad and grad school without needing a loan, but just as I started to think I might retire at 60, something about the shape of the object stopped me cold.

Below me, I could see a slightly bulbous knob that appeared to taper down further into the soil. The object was a creamy white color that I, unfortunately, recognized.

It was a bone, and given my luck with jobsites and bodies, I wasn't going to bank on the fact that some poor dog had met its end under the chicken coop. "Santiago?" I called as loudly as I could while trying to remain calm.

Clearly, my voice had not conveyed calmness because he sprinted around the house from the firepit. He came to an abrupt stop when he saw what I was staring at. "Is that what I think it is?"

I shook my head. "I hope not."

2

Unfortunately, neither my dreams of the Roadshow nor my hopes that this wasn't a human body were panning out. Santiago had quickly determined that, as best he could tell, I had found the knee-end of a human femur. So we were sitting around waiting for the coroner to arrive so that she could extract the rest of the remains.

Jackie had invited us to wait inside with her, but none of us had been much in the mood for polite conversation. So Santi and I had taken the huge, ice-filled glasses of Pepsi she'd offered and gone to sprawl in the grass while we waited, nestling the glasses into taller tufts of grass so they wouldn't tip over.

I was lying on my back with my phone creating a sunshade for my eyes while I tried to begin the research I needed to do anyway to establish the provenance of the wood I hoped to sell. I knew that I'd be spending a lot more time looking into the person whose body we had just found, but right now, I needed to keep my mind busy, especially since Jackie had told me she didn't know much about the previous owners.

My explorations had already revealed that the farm had

been in existence for well over 150 years, but I hadn't bothered to dig into the ownership yet. Now, though, I was trying to figure out who had owned the place before Jackie. Fortunately, Octonia had digitized the past ten years of deed records, and the date when Jackie bought the place was just six years ago.

With a few taps of my finger, I had the name of the previous owner: Jonathan Boykins. He had lived here for at least four years before selling the place – that much I could tell because his name wasn't included as a purchaser for the property in that decade's worth of records.

His name was unusual, especially around here, so I was able to track him down fairly quickly with a Google search. Apparently, he was an elite cabinetmaker who specialized in custom-made pieces for homes. His website included images of beautiful wardrobes and spans of kitchen cabinets that made me a little envious of their owners. Okay, a lot envious.

A few more taps of my finger brought up his Facebook profile, and from the images he had made public I could see he wore a long, graying beard and appeared to enjoy wearing leather kilts at Renaissance faires and the like. He seemed friendly enough, and I didn't see any affiliations on his page to suggest he was a serial killer, a member of the KKK, or a Holocaust denier. Believe it or not, I'd met two of those three in person when researching other projects in the area, and I didn't want a repeat of those conversations. Also, serial killers weren't high on my list of people to talk to.

I turned my head toward Santi, who appeared to be taking a nap in the afternoon sun, and said, "I found the previous owner. If I don't mention the bone, do you mind if I reach out on the pretense of research about the chicken coop?"

The corner of Santi's mouth twitched up. "I appreciate the courtesy of the ask, Paisley, but we both know you can't resist a research conundrum when you come upon one. Go right ahead." He turned his head and looked at me. "But yeah, don't mention the bone."

I nodded and opened Messenger on my phone. My note to Boykins was very brief and just explained that I was doing some research about the property he used to own down by Octonia Creek and wondered if he would mind talking with me about it.

With my research process at a dead end for the moment, I put my phone into my pocket and rolled over to lay my head on Santiago's chest after determining I had enough chicken dust in my hair already to not worry about the coating on his clothing. "Do you ever think I'm bad luck?" It was a question I carried around with me all the time.

Santiago didn't even pause. "Nope," he said as he put a warm hand on my back. "These people would be dead no matter what, and the fact that you find them and recover their stories – I think they're pretty lucky folks."

I felt a little glow in my chest. I guess he was right. If I didn't do what I did, no one would know where these people were, and the stories of their deaths would remain hidden. I didn't know if I could take any credit for bringing people closure, but I hoped I was doing right by history and its people to help preserve not only buildings but the stories of the people who had lived and loved in them, too.

I sighed. Still, I couldn't help but feel a little weird about the fact that I was uncovering – quite literally, in many cases – the darkest sides of Octonia history. In the past year or two that I'd been doing this work, I'd heard from more than a few local folks that I needed to stop meddling, stop digging up the past. "Leave it where it lays," one man had said. Some folks didn't like secrets being brought to light for various reasons. Mostly because some people just couldn't handle uncomfortable topics of discussion.

Often I couldn't help but wonder if some of these people

were trying to scare me off my work just so I wouldn't be able to tie them to something unsavory in their family's history. I had decided long ago, however, to not let other people's fears become my own. This was my work – to tell the truth – and I was going to keep doing that for as long as I could.

"Thanks," I said to Santiago as I snuggled deeper into his arm. "How much longer will the coroner be?" I asked.

At that moment, tires crunched over the gravel driveway. "Sounds like not much longer at all," he said before rearing his head up to kiss the top of my head. "Come on. Let's get her back here so we can see what we're dealing with."

We stood up from the warm grass, and I followed him around to the front of the house to greet Alexandra Chu, the new county coroner. She'd moved up from Richmond a couple months back, and we'd become fast friends because her daughter Olivia and Sawyer had become besties at a law enforcement picnic over the summer. The two of them played together at least a couple times a week, so Alex and I had spent a lot of time watching them play while we sipped sweet tea or a little white wine.

"Hi, Alex," I said as she pulled her messenger bag out of her van. "Sorry to bring you out this late in the day."

"Part of the gig," she said as she gave first me and then Santiago a fist bump. "Show me what we've got?"

Jackie joined us as we went back to the site of the chicken coop, and while the three of us watched, Alex finished clearing the soil around the bone I'd found and pulled it gently from the ground.

"Human femur," she said definitively. "Probably a young man. Maybe 20, 25. I'll know more in the lab" – she looked down at the ground – "or if we find more remains." She knelt and moved back the top couple of inches of soil around her. "We need to excavate the whole site."

I groaned and sent an apologetic smile toward Jackie. "I'm

so sorry, Jack. A simple project has become this whole big thing."

"Are you kidding? This is the most exciting event to happen to me in a long time. Let's get digging." She picked up a long-handled shovel from the stack of tools I'd dropped off earlier in the week and started to dig.

"Slow your roll there, woman," Alex said with a smile and wink. "Pun intended. Let's get a grid out first. We want to be sure we know where the remains came from."

Jackie chuckled. "Sorry. Right. I was a little overeager, huh?" She glanced at Santi. "Does that make me a suspect?"

"Do you want to be a suspect?" he said with one raised eyebrow. "Be careful what you wish for."

"Point taken," Jackie said gamely and pushed the head of the shovel into the grass next to the coop lot. "How can I help?"

"Grab that string, Pais," Alex said. "You two can do the east-west grid, and Santiago and I will do north-south."

I stared at her without moving.

It was Santi's turn to chuckle now. "You do the long side, Pais. We'll get the short side."

"Got it," I said, a little embarrassed by my absolute inability to tell direction without a map. I took the string Alex handed me and gave one end to Jackie. "You hold it, and I'll stretch it?"

"Works for me," Jackie said as she positioned herself at one corner of the small square of bare earth.

A few minutes later, we had the space gridded out with white twine, and Jackie and I watched while Alex and Santiago each took a square and began to dig. It was only a couple of minutes before Santiago said, "I have a bone."

I looked over to where he was digging, about four feet from the original site, and sure enough, there at the surface was the same whitish sheen of bone. He had the bone removed in a moment, and Alex said "rib" with such casualness that my mind called forth barbecue before I shuddered and forced myself to remember it was a human rib bone. This was getting more morbid by the second.

Within an hour or so, they had uncovered a dozen more bones, including a jaw bone, and it was clear that the process of digging out the rest of the site was going to be more than we all could handle in the remaining couple hours of daylight. Santiago called in his deputies, Savannah Wilson and the new guys Brett Millon and Terrance Andrews, and Alex asked her assistant to come, too.

With the rest of them there, they got a couple of feet down into each square. When they were done, we had – according to Alex – most of the bones of a male skeleton, adult but young. "We'll come back tomorrow and dig a little deeper to see if any missing bones are here, but we have the major ones," she told us as she climbed up out of what was now a sizable pit in Jackie's yard.

"Did animals spread the bones around like this?" Jackie said as she wiped a solid streak of mud across her forehead. "I mean, why else would they be so widely distributed?"

I had to admit I had the same question, but unfortunately, I didn't think the answer was Jackie's pack of hungry raccoons. This seemed more systematic than that.

Alex shook her head. "No, this wasn't animals. This body was fully dissected and then buried, piece by piece." She stared at the partially assembled skeleton she had laid out on a body bag. "There are no teeth marks, and from what I can see, no knife marks, either. It looks like this person was fully decomposed before their skeleton was taken apart and then buried here."

I slid my hands down my face and suppressed a moan. Just when I thought people couldn't get even more messed up … "How can we help?" I said, pushing down my disgust and focusing on the reality of a human being lying there before me.

"Yeah, what can we do?" Jackie echoed.

"Do you have a couple of tarps we can put over the site?" Alex asked. "I don't think it's going to rain, but I don't want to take any chances."

"Got it," Jackie said and headed out toward her garage by the house. When she came back, we spread the blue sheets over the ground and laid some heavy rocks on the corners to keep them in place.

"I'll be back first thing tomorrow," Alex said, "with a team to finish up. Would you like me to call first?"

Jackie shook her head. "Nope. I'll be up early and have coffee and scones for you whenever you get here." She sighed. "Not sure I'll sleep at all tonight."

I nodded. "I know what you mean." I looked at Santiago. "Do you need to stay and talk with Alex? I can walk home." I glanced across the railroad tracks to my house that was there in the slanted light of evening.

He looked at Alex, who said, "I'll call as soon as I find out anything."

Santi nodded. "I'll keep the phone handy." As if that was different from usual. "Thanks, Alex. Thanks, Jackie. See you all tomorrow."

My hands were filthy, and I really needed a good shower. But I needed the comfort of Santiago's hand in mind more, so as soon as we were up the drive a bit, I intertwined my fingers with his. He squeezed them and said, "How does pizza sound?"

"Perfect," I said as I glanced at my watch. "Dad and Lucille are coming, so we can ask them to pick it up when they bring Sawyer home."

He glanced at me and took a quick breath. "What if Saw stayed with them tonight? They could do a sleepover and take him to school. I think you could use a night off."

I sighed. I could use a night off, and while I didn't usually allow Sawyer sleepovers on weeknights, I also didn't usually find disassembled bodies under chicken coops. "That's a good idea. I'll call Lucille."

The call with my stepmother was short and direct. She thought it a great idea for Sawyer to stay over, and when she put Saw on the phone, he was ecstatic. "Baba and I just made pretzels, and now I can eat yours too."

"You can, but you better save me one for when I pick you up at school tomorrow?" I softened my voice. "You're okay with this?"

"Yep," he said, and then I heard the phone drop.

A moment later, Lucille said, "I guess he's done."

"I guess he is," I said with a laugh. "Thanks."

"Absolutely, and we'll see you at Jackie's after we drop him off. I'll bring coffee cake." She disconnected before I had a chance to tell her that Jackie was making scones, but maybe that was just as well. We could probably use a good selection of baked goods for this intense work.

At home, Santiago and I took our turns in the shower while we waited for a pizza with extra cheese, ham, and pineapple to arrive. Sawyer had recently started to detest pineapple, most days anyway, so this was a treat. When the food arrived with cinnamon-frosted breadsticks, I thanked Santiago for the extra treat and tucked into the food.

While we ate on the couch, we watched *Love is Blind* and made ruthless fun of the contestants while also picking who we wanted to win. It was a perfect way to blow off steam. But after a couple of episodes, we both grew quiet, and when I said I thought I needed to do some research, Santiago turned off the TV, took out my laptop, and put it on my lap. "I'll take notes," he said as he picked up the pen and paper I kept on the table by the couch.

I doubted I'd heard from Jonathan Boykins because the message had probably gone into that mysterious shadow-folder for Facebook messages, but I thought it best to check there.

Surprisingly enough, he had written, and he said he was happy to talk about the "old Cavanaugh place," as he called it, whenever I'd like. He lived just over in Orange now and said he could meet up anytime.

Santiago wrote down his number, and I texted him right away to see if we could get together for lunch the next day. He replied immediately and with enthusiasm. *Definitely. Is the burger place by the train station okay? Have you tried their fries?*

I had indeed tried their fries and loved them, so I confirmed noon for burgers.

"Okay, so we have one lead," I said.

"Now you're chasing down leads?" Santiago said with a smirk. "I thought that was my job."

"Researchers follow leads, too, I'll have you know," I said. "Law enforcement doesn't own the copyright to the term *lead*." I rolled my eyes.

He laughed. "True. But we do own the role of *investigation*, wouldn't you agree?"

"Fair enough. So what if I just investigate the place, and you investigate the body?" I looked at him with raised eyebrows. "Deal?"

"Deal." He pointed to the computer. "Okay, researcher, what can we find?"

"Well, Boykins mentioned the name Cavanaugh, so I think we should dig there." I pulled up the images of the historic maps I consulted all the time, opened the oldest one, and zoomed in on Jackie's location. "Sometimes on these maps, the owners of properties are identified." But this 1805 map didn't have a name anywhere near the house structure marked there.

We looked at the next one from 1838, and as I'd remembered, Jackie's house was there and next to it was the name *Cavanaugh* written in script right across the area that would become Jackie's land. I pushed out the focus of the map and saw that there was another Cavanaugh just up the hill from

Jackie's place, and then I pulled up the plat map for that area in the current GIS system. I was hoping that maybe a Cavanaugh still owned that land, but it wasn't the case. We had to go another way.

For the next hour, Santiago and I searched the early census records for the nineteenth century, and we didn't find much until 1840. But there, in the Octonia lists, we found a list for two men – Isaac and Micah Cavanaugh. They were each listed first in their households with women about their same ages and several children in each house. Given that the men were roughly the same age – in their early 30s – I guessed they were probably brothers. Since they were on the census on adjoining pages, it appeared the census taker had written down their notes consecutively, something that indicated they were probably neighbors, too. It seemed likely that we had found our Cavanaughs.

"But which brother lived at Jackie's place?" Santi asked.

I shook my head. "I don't know yet, but I should be able to figure it out pretty quickly tomorrow at the clerk's office." I opened up a new browser tab and said, "Okay, last thing."

"Is that your way of telling me I need to pry away your laptop after this?" Santi said.

"Yes, because like my son, I can do twenty-five 'last things' if I'm not held to one." I pulled up the newspaper research site and did a quick search for Isaac Cavanaugh. Nothing came up, but when I typed in his brother's name, a string of results ran down the page. A quick skim of the article titles told me that this "one last thing" might not be a brief one.

"Cavanaugh Beaten for Violating Temperance Order," one headline read. I clicked open the article, and Santi and I read. Apparently, Micah Cavanaugh had operated a tavern just up the road a piece from where he lived, and some local temperance advocates had caught him after he closed up one night. They'd beaten him nearly to death.

The article contained a photo, and when I zoomed in, I was hit with a sense of recognition. "The tavern was in the old train station," I said and looked at Santi with delighted awareness.

He, however, stared at me like I was speaking one of the alien languages from *The Mandalorian.*

"Oh, right. Across the train tracks, where the florist shop is." When he nodded, I continued, "That's the old train station. But this picture tells me it was the Cavanaugh Tavern before it was the train station. That is so cool."

Santi studied the picture. "Okay, nice local history, but what does that tell us about Jackie's place?"

"Well, it seems likely that Micah Cavanaugh lived there, for one. Although I can't be sure of that until I look at the land records, since his brother lived so close." I backed up to the list of search results and picked another to read as I continued. "But it also means that Micah Cavanaugh had run afoul of some of the more hard-core temperance folks. People took their position on that issue very seriously."

Santiago nodded. "It seems so." He pointed toward the screen. "What does that one say?"

I scanned the article from 1833 quickly. "Seems like Cavanaugh's wife ran into some trouble, too." I read out loud, "'Millie Cavanaugh, wife of tavern keeper Micah Cavanaugh, suffered a serious fall from her horse today when three young men chased her through the woods when she was out for a spring ride.'"

"Someone chased a woman down when she was on a horse. That sounds terrifying." Santiago shook his head.

It did sound terrifying. Given the way women had to be attentive about some of the men in the world, I had always feared a man following me home at night, but this seemed worse. At least I'd have my car – but on a horse, where could she go, and how fast? Chills ran up my arms. "Says she broke her arm and had considerable bruising."

Santiago sighed. "She's lucky she didn't break her neck."

I nodded adamantly. Horses were one of those animals that I loved to see run and could snuggle all day ... but I wasn't about to get on the back of one. Those suckers are strong. Once again, I was glad I lived in the twenty-first century, not the nineteenth.

"Okay, there's a lot more stories here, but I need to sleep." I started to close the laptop.

"Just one more," he said.

I looked at him out of the corner of my eye. "It's bit you, hasn't it?"

"What?"

"The research bug," I said with a sly smile as I opened the computer I had never intended to close anyway.

3

Santi and I stayed up way too late reading articles about the Cavanaughs. Apparently, they were the nineteenth century equivalent of the contemporary couple who just didn't find it necessary to abide by societal rules. I liked them for that and imagined that if they lived now, they'd probably plant their front yard in wildflowers, paint their house lavender, and insist on letting their children run around the yard naked. I went to sleep thinking I'd like to be friends with them.

But when the alarm went off at five a.m., both of us groaned so loudly that we startled Beauregard, who was sleeping between us, and he dug all ten of his claws into my calf. That woke me up all the way, and I headed downstairs to make coffee. I knew Jackie said she'd have some for us, but I needed fuel just for the trip over there.

By the time we walked over, leaving Santi's cruiser in my driveway, Alex and her team were already working in the early morning light. Jackie had set up a card table off to the side, and an insulated thermos of coffee sat there with sugar, creamer, and the most amazing-looking blueberry scones I'd ever seen.

I wanted to be the person who went right to work, but I was the person who went right to eat. Only when I had consumed an entire scone did I ask Alex what I could do. She pointed toward Brett, who was taking notes and affixing labels to bags, and had me take over from him.

For the next hour, I watched our little team lift scoop by scoop of dirt out into clear plastic trays and sift through it with gloved fingers to be sure they didn't miss tiny bones. I noticed there was nothing to be recorded in any of the corners of the grid and I began to wonder why, until I realized that was right where the footers for the coop had been.

"Alex, I'm not seeing anything in the corners."

Alex looked at me closely. "What are you thinking?"

"It looks to me like the footers were left in place when the bones were buried."

The building had sat up on some ten- or fifteen-pound pieces of bedrock Santiago and I had moved out of the way when we'd finished taking down the shed. The rocks had been heavy, and a couple of them had required that we work together to move them. They were not objects that could be casually thrown aside.

"I don't know if this is true, but I think someone could have picked up the coop, buried the bones, and then put it back," I said to everyone, as they looked at me and stretched their backs. "There are no bones here where the foundation stones were, which makes me think the bones were put here after the coop was built."

Alex furrowed her brow. "Really? That's a lot of work to conceal a body."

"More work than burying each bone separately?" Santi asked.

"I guess not," Alex said with a shake of her head that brought a lock of her straight black hair out of the bun at the back of her head. "So you're thinking someone really wanted to hide this body?"

I nodded. "I think so. The floor of the coop was off the ground, but not by much, maybe three or four inches. So there's no way the person could have gotten under there to bury the bones." I studied the plot of land in front of me. "But if the bones had been there before the coop was built, I'd think we'd find bones everywhere, even under the foundation stones, maybe even outside the grid."

Alex nodded and looked around. "At this point, we're only missing a couple of small finger bones, which we will either find as we finish up or that were actually carried off by scavengers."

"So that means the whole body was within the space of the coop?" Jackie asked.

"Yes, I'd say so." Alex looked at me. "We need to know when this coop was built."

I agreed as I stepped up and out of the hole. "I'm on it." I had carried my laptop over from my house, and Jackie gave me her newest Wi-Fi password. Within minutes, I was back on the old map sites looking for anything that might indicate a chicken coop. But the building didn't show up at all until more recent aerial photos of the area. This wasn't unusual because maps usually just indicated property ownership and not the placement of structures. But in this case, I wished the mapmakers had been a bit more thorough. Now, this research was going to have to be the paper kind, at the clerk's office. If we were lucky, we'd find some records of the buildings on the property.

Dad and Lucille showed up just as I was leaving. They let me know that Sawyer had gone to bed easily and gotten up without any trouble. Going into school had been a bit of a challenge because he hadn't wanted to miss out on what we were all doing, but when he saw his friends, he'd made up his mind that whatever the grown-ups were doing could wait. "'It's okay, Baba,' he told me," Lucille said. "'I'll play with you next month.'" She smiled.

"Well, I hope you have big plans for next month, then," I said with a smile. "Thanks for taking care of him."

"Everything okay here?" Dad asked.

I nodded. "As okay as it can be. If you guys want to help, they're trying to double-check for anything we missed. But I have to go get cleaned up and head into town to do some research." I thought about inviting Lucille along, but research at the clerk's office could be tedious. I didn't want to feel pressured about how much time I was taking.

"We'll do what we can," Lucille said as she swung a cake carrier up into both of her hands. "But first, sustenance." She headed over to where Jackie had set up the scones, which had been plundered down to crumbs, and lifted the cover off her two-tiered coffee cake. I had never seen such cinnamon goodness, and I was mighty tempted to grab a piece for the road. But I decided against it in favor of a cup of coffee with Mika before I went to the clerk's office. I needed a minute with my bestie to just take in all that was happening.

After a quick shower, a headband, and a drive into town, I swung by the coffee shop for two cappuccinos and headed across the street. Mika was in the middle of ringing up a customer, so I smiled and waved the coffee cup above my head before settling into the Cozy Nook.

A month or so ago, Mika had splurged on a magazine subscription to *What Women Create*, and the latest issue was on the table. The cover showed what looked like jellyfish, but when I opened the magazine, I saw that the artist had crafted those beauties from translucent fabric. I wasn't a big ocean person, but if I were, I'd be scooping some of those up to decorate my house.

By the time I finished reading all about the artist's work,

Mika had completed the sale and joined me for our beverages. "What brings you by?" she said as she tapped her cup against mine.

"Just really wanted to see your face," I said. "It's been a wild couple of days."

"I'll say," she said with a shake of her head. "Catch me up."

I told her everything I hadn't mentioned in my intermittent texts over the past couple of days, and when I was done, she sighed. "Whoa."

"Yep," I said as I drank the last of my capp. "Now, I'm headed to the clerk's office to see what I can dig up in the property records and what I can find about the Cavanaughs."

"Good luck," Mika said. "Want to do lunch?"

"Can't. I'm meeting Jonathan Boykins. Bring you something after?" I said.

"Nah, I'll grab something. Mrs. Stephenson will be in at noon, and I'm going to need a break, I think." She smiled as a group of six women came into the store. "Looks like we're going to have a busy morning."

I smiled and waved as I made my way past the new customers, who were already raving over the silk yarns Mika had just added to her inventory. She was going to have a good morning, and she deserved it.

The clerk's office was just up the street, so I walked along Main and enjoyed the sun from its lower angle in the early fall sky. The heat was still up and would be for a few more weeks, but when the sun started tilting down, I began to dream of autumn. Cooler days, chilly nights, and bonfires galore.

Once inside the air conditioning of the clerk's office, I got right to work with the deed books and quickly spun back through the decades to record everyone who had owned the property. Jackie most recently, then before her, Boykins for close to ten years. Before that, a string of owners had farmed the land, which was a considerably larger parcel pre-1955. I made notes of everyone's names, but it wasn't until the 1830s that I found the name I was looking for.

Micah Cavanaugh had bought the land from someone named Burnley in 1832. The property totaled twenty-eight acres and contained no structures, and while there was no image of the formal plat, the surveyor's notes indicated, as best I could tell, that it ran up the hillside toward where I presumed his brother Isaac lived.

I didn't find anything unusual in the deed transfer. Micah paid and the previous owner sold. No stipulations or specific notes. No trade of goods, just a straight-up cash transaction. But the fact that there were no structures on the land told me that the chicken coop couldn't date any earlier than 1832, which was good information for both my business records and for the murder investigation.

To be thorough, I flipped back and traced the deed back a few more decades only to discover that it was the Burnley family who had gotten the original land grant. So in essence, the Cavanaughs were only the second owners of this particular parcel, notwithstanding the Monacan people who would have called it home for centuries before that.

With that information in mind, I went to go see what further information I could locate on any of the previous owners. If I had been very systematic, I would have started with the Burnley family and looked at their wills and other records, but the newspaper articles from the night before were in the front of my mind. So I started with the Cavanaughs, specifically Micah and Millie (Millicent) Cavanaugh.

I found them quickly in the census records when I turned on my laptop, and within a few minutes I had their family tree sketched out for several further generations, right until the early 1900s. But it was Millie and Micah that had really captured my attention, so I turned to the will books before doing more of their family genealogy.

And that's when things got really interesting. In 1849, Micah Cavanaugh was declared insane, by legal definition, and committed to the Western State Hospital in Staunton. I didn't know much about that particular institution (the later DeJarnette Hospital was more famous since the founder insisted on forced sterilizations for his patients), but I knew enough about mental health care in nineteenth-century America to imagine that Micah had not had a great experience there.

The records didn't note what Micah's ailment was, but my previous research made me believe that he could have had anything from epilepsy to a hand tremor to sociopathic tendencies. Any of those and a number of other illnesses and ailments could have gotten him committed, as could the false testimony of witnesses who harbored ill against him. Clearly, I had some more research on Micah to do.

But first, I wanted to see what I could find about Millie. Given that their oldest son, Obadiah, wasn't yet of age when his father went away, only fourteen, Millie would have assumed some level of control of the farm, maybe with assigned guardians to give her the assistance that those of her sex "naturally lacked." This part of our nation's history irked me to no end, as did many others. As a woman who had, on occasion, been a victim of the vestiges of this patriarchal hogwash, I often got more worked up about the treatment of women across time than about anything else. That was really saying something because I got worked up about how a lot of people have been treated in history.

When I turned to find Millie's will, which was recorded twenty-five years after the record of her husband's institutionalization, I had my second big surprise for the day. Millie had kept the family farm, had run it herself for twenty-five years, and had willed it to her daughter, Jemima, when she died. I did a little happy dance right there at the high shelves in the clerk's office. A man doing deed research on the computer smiled a little but left me to my own celebration.

Before I moved on to see what Jemima had done with the place, I looked up Micah Cavanaugh's will, which was recorded in the same will book as the record of his commitment. He'd died just four years after being committed, and because his assets had already been transferred to his wife, his will record was brief and simply noted his death with a reference back to the record of his earlier institutionalization. Nothing more to find there.

I was at a crossroads of research again. I could dig into what had made someone commit Micah Cavanaugh; I could research Millie and what she had done as a landowner; or I could travel down the family history timeline and see what Jemima had been up to. If I knew the date of the bones we'd found, this choice would be easy, but given that basically anyone at any time could have moved the coop and buried the skeleton, I decided to focus on Micah first and then Millie, since I'd likely find more information about one if I found something about the other.

Given that Micah had lived only slightly longer than four years at Western State, I wasn't confident that I could find much about his time there, but his time in the hospital had covered a year the census was taken. So I went back to my computer and pulled up his name there. Sure enough, he was listed as residing at the Western State Hospital, and, fortunately for me, the census taker had noted that he suffered from catatonia.

My reading in Victorian literature had introduced me to the idea of a catatonic state when I was quite young, since "frail" women seemed to slip into those states at the slightest disturbance in some of the novels of that time. But a quick bit of internet research informed me that this kind of mental condition could come about for many reasons, including head injury, traumatic experience, or a mental illness like bipolar disorder.

So Micah could have actually been quite ill, or he could have been made catatonic by the rather brutal treatment methods in state hospitals at the time. Without digging into actual medical records, I couldn't tell.

I jotted down a note to ask Xzanthia Nicholas, the director of our local historical society, if she knew where the Western State Hospital records were kept. She might be able to give me some guidance on how to find out more about Micah's condition.

That path of inquiry blocked for now, I looked up more information on Millie. In the 1850, 1860, and 1870 censuses, she was listed as head of household. Four of her children moved out as they got older, but Jemima, the middle girl of three, stayed on with her mother and was still listed as living with her in 1870. I expected this might be why Jemima inherited the farm. Loyalty holds a lot of sway for most of us.

I did some further searches for Millie in the various records at the clerk's office, but I didn't find anything in the chancery cases or the various and sundry church and other records on the shelves. I made myself another note to go back and read more of the newspaper articles about her and Micah in hopes that they might tell me something about either or both of them.

But it was Jemima who held the most promise for me in the last half hour I had before I met Jonathan Boykins for lunch. I sat back down at my laptop and went into the census records again. Jemima was listed in each census as single and living in that particular census district all the way through 1930. No one lived with her, no husband or other woman, no children. Just her for at least fifty years.

Twice she was listed as being a schoolteacher, and I couldn't help but think about the previous schoolteachers I'd researched. I wondered what it was about women who chose to teach for many years; since teachers generally didn't continue to teach after marriage, it seemed likely that they were interested in pursuing life independent of a husband's influence.

In 1934, I found Jemima's death record. Cause of death: myocardial infarction. She'd died of a heart attack. That's not the worst way to go for a woman who was eighty-nine years old. She had lived a good life, and I had to stop myself from thinking she must have been lonely. I didn't know that. All I knew was that she'd lived alone, according to the records, for around seventy years.

A quick glance at my watch told me I had ten minutes to get to the restaurant to meet Boykins, so I opened my deed notes just to confirm what I suspected. Yes, the property had passed to the next owners in 1934, after Jemima's death. She had willed it to a nephew, it seemed, and apparently, he had sold it the next year, probably because his residence was in New Jersey. That's when the Cavanaughs' ties to the home place ended. I couldn't help feeling a bit sad about that.

WHEN I ARRIVED at the restaurant, the woman at the front podium pointed me to a booth in the back, where a man who looked much like his photos on Facebook stood as I approached. "Paisley?" he asked.

"Jonathan," I said, following his cue about the use of first names. I smiled, and his face crinkled into a gentle ocean of wrinkles that made me think of some combination of Santa Claus and the Highlander. Okay, maybe his affinity for kilts was what made me think of the Highlander.

He reached out and grabbed me for a hug tight enough to crack my back. It felt great, if a little startling. "I'm so glad to meet you," he said. "Let's get food, and then we can talk about why you're so interested in my old chicken coop."

I ordered a Cobb salad with extra bacon (always), and Jonathan got himself the best burger on the menu. I had to admit to some envy of his choice after I had gone (sort of) healthy. But I had been eating on the far side of the moon in terms of my health lately, and I knew my system needed something green, much as I tried to tell myself differently.

Our orders out of the way, Jonathan got right to business. "So, did you find something valuable in the coop?"

I stared at him, my mouth slightly open for a minute, as I tried to figure out how he knew. Had word about the bones already begun to spread through town?

He tilted his head and looked at me. "Oh, right. I googled you," he said with a broad smile. "You do architectural salvage, right? I've been bingeing your newsletters this morning. You've found some really cool stuff." He lowered his voice. "And some sad stuff, too."

I let out a slow stream of air. "I have. And thanks for clarifying. I'm not used to being recognized, I guess." I didn't dare admit that I thought some of that "sad stuff" he'd mentioned was what had scared me about his statement. "Unfortunately, I didn't find much of value at your old coop," I said, hoping that I wasn't crossing a moral line by defining *value* as monetary.

He shook his head. "Too bad. I was hoping it would be a windfall for you."

This time, I looked at him carefully, surprised that he would so easily grant me rights to something that could have belonged in his family. "You wouldn't try to claim it if I found some piece of rare pottery or a fabulous coin or something?"

"Why would I? I sold that place and all that went with it. Sure, it's sentimental to me, given that it belonged to me and my family for so long, but I don't stake claim to what isn't mine." He smiled up at the waiter as he brought our meals and then took a large bite of his burger before letting his eyes roll back in his head in delight. "Oh my lord, that's good."

"Best burgers around," I said with a sigh as I picked up my fork and speared a piece of lettuce and then bacon. The bacon helped, but not much. "Well, that's mighty admirable. You and your family lived in that house, I gather from the land records."

At this, he threw back his head and laughed. "Me and my family. Oh, woman, you are funny. I ain't got any kids, a wife neither. Just me and my bachelor self. Been that way my whole life. Love it, too, just in case you might be getting all pitying on me or something." He snagged another bite of his burger and groaned in delight.

I smiled. I appreciated a person who appreciated their food. "Oh, I'm sorry. I shouldn't have presumed. But I'm confused. You said you and your family lived in that house for a long time."

He shook his head. "No, I said the place had belonged to me and my family for a long time. I'd hoped to pass it down again, but no kids and no siblings." He paused and glanced out the window at Main Street. "Glad that nice woman lives there now, though, and I'm thrilled you're looking into the place's history. Aunt Jemima would be so happy."

I dropped my fork. "Jemima Cavanaugh was your aunt?" I stared at him as I waited for him to finish his bite of burger.

"You have done your homework," he said with another grin. "Yep, great-great-aunt, actually. According to family stories, she was a hoot. She could hit a spittoon from fifty feet away." He winked at me. "Rumor has it, too, that she may have been a spinster but she was no stranger to the joys of the flesh, if you know what I mean."

I laughed. "Really?" The sad and lonely picture that I'd conjured up of Jemima had been completely off, apparently. "She sounds amazing."

"She basically saved my mother's life. My grandmother wasn't exactly the most attentive mother, and she'd leave my mom with Aunt Jemima for days at a time." Jonathan shook his head. "At first, Mom said she hated it. All the chores and the isolation, but eventually, it became her safe place. Jemima taught her all about gardening and caring for chickens. Eventually, Mama moved in with her, took care of her until she died."

"Sounds like they had a special bond," I said as I imagined the old woman and the young girl out together in the garden, harvesting and then putting up tomatoes for the winter. It was a vision I had for Sawyer and me, too, and the idea of it endeared me to Jemima even more.

"They did," Jonathan said as he stared out the window toward Main Street again. "I said Jemima saved my mom, but I think Mom saved her, too. The story goes that not long before Mom moved in, some man jilted Jemima hard. The family still doesn't talk about it much, but Mom always said she wished she'd known Jemima before Johnny broke her down."

I took a deep breath as the possibilities for what that could mean raised goose bumps on my arms. "Any idea what Johnny's last name was?"

Jonathan shook his head. "No idea. But if you find out, I'd love to know." He cracked his neck and looked at me. "So what can I tell you about the coop?"

I wasn't sure if he was making an intentional change of subject or simply trying to honor my time and the purpose of our meeting, but it didn't matter. I was getting itchy about telling him about the bones, and that wasn't my place. Plus, it really would help me to know more about the building for both that purpose and my own research.

"Well, do you, by chance, know when it was built?" I asked.

"Not exactly, but I'm guessing it was when the first Cavanaughs built their house." He shrugged. "I think it was pretty standard to have chickens back then, but then you'd know more about that than I would." He smiled at me.

I took out my pen and made some notes. "I could get a dendrological analysis of the wood, but I'm thinking that might be a little overdoing it for a chicken coop." I laughed as I thought about the expense of that report versus what I could get for the wood. "Do you know when your family built the house? What year?"

"Oh yeah, that's easy. The house was built in 1837. That was always a point of pride in the family, that we've had this house for almost two hundred years now." He sat up a little straighter, as if the pride was etched into his bones, which I supposed it was.

I wrote down the date and then took a deep breath. "Are you a descendant of Micah?" I asked without lifting my eyes from the notebook page.

"Nope," Jonathan said, and I looked up. "Isaac. Uncle Micah was the crazy one." He winced. "Sorry. I don't say that casually. He was actually committed to an asylum."

"I think I read something about that," I said noncommittally. "Do you know what his ailment was?" I knew what I'd read about catatonia, but I also knew medical records could be wildly inaccurate – even intentionally inaccurate.

Jonathan studied my face for a minute. "The family stories are pretty wide-ranging, from something like epilepsy with seizures so bad that they torched his brain, to much more terrible things like the idea that he was a psychopath and hurt his wife."

I took a slow, deep breath. "Wow. That's hard, whatever the case." I tapped my pen on my paper for a second. "What's your take?"

He looked out the window again. "Probably somewhere in between. I imagine he had something wrong with him, maybe something that made him turn mean or just have a hard time coping. But I feel like something as intense as being a homicidal maniac, if you'll excuse the expression, would have left a more permanent mark." He looked back at me. "You know, on history or in our family."

I sighed and nodded. I wasn't sure it hadn't left that mark, but since I couldn't bring myself to tell Jonathan about the bones on his family's homestead, I kept my mouth shut.

Without another word, Jonathan slapped his hands down on the table, smiled at me, and squeezed my shoulder with a firm hand as he walked toward the door. "Talk to you soon, Paisley," he said as he stepped out onto the street.

For a few moments, I sat twisted in my seat and staring at the door he had just walked through. I didn't know if his abrupt departure was a result of our conversation, a sudden realization he had about where he needed to be, or just his personality. I was inclined to think it was the latter, but who knew?

I gathered up my things and headed across the street to the historical society. I had a lot more digging to do if I was going to figure out the mysteries of the Cavanaugh family, but at least I knew now when the house had been built.

4

As soon as I started looking into the records that Ms. Nicholas dug out for me in the historical society archives, I found a discrepancy about the house's date. According to a local 1835 map of the area, the house was already standing at that date. Two years wasn't much of a difference, though, so I wasn't too concerned. I could just say "around 1837" and keep the family story solid.

But then, Ms. Nicholas put me onto a trove of hospital records from Western State. Mary Baldwin College held the collection, and they'd digitized most of it. It was a researcher's paradise.

Immediately, though, some of the records made me question whether Micah Cavanaugh had ever been in a position to build a house. The medical records I found digitized in a local university's archives indicated that Micah had been a patient on and off at Western State from 1825 on, meaning that he'd been in and out of the hospital for more than a decade before he was formally committed. It was hard for me to fathom that a man who had health troubles so severe that they involved a day's journey over the mountains to a hospital could have afforded to build a house, much less done the labor himself, as would have been the norm for someone in his economic class at the time.

But he had run a tavern, so somehow he'd managed to own a business. Maybe his health was good, by and large, but had some really nasty moments. I knew people who lived like that now, and it seemed so very hard.

A little further research made it clear that this was exactly the situation. I could see from the treatment records that Micah had suffered from a severe form of epilepsy, one that frequently gave him what we now call grand mal seizures. The hospital had tried various medications and treatments for him, but nothing seemed to have slowed down the massive storms of electricity in his brain. While it wasn't definitively noted that his seizure disorder had led to his catatonia, everything I read led me to believe that was a good possibility.

I wasn't yet in a place to give Jonathan the news that his family bloodline contained a history of epilepsy, but I did look forward to the day when I could tell him that Micah wasn't, as far as I could tell, a psychopath.

But all this information led me back to the questions that had started to form earlier. How had Micah supported his family as he got more and more unwell? Who had taken over his tavern? What had Millie done during this time? It was that last question that really had me curious.

Not for the first time and surely not for the last time, I cursed the patriarchal system that left women not only without our own names but also without much formal record in history. The fact that Millie lived a hundred years before she could have even had the right to vote meant the historical record about her existence was probably very scant. But given that I'd found an article about her horse accident in a very cursory newspaper search, I had a little hope that she had been, as the saying goes, "badly behaved" enough to make recorded history more often.

The question was how to search for the records of that

behavior. I was just beginning to compile my list of possible sources when Mika texted and asked if I could come over.

My friend so rarely asked for things from me that I almost ran out of the door. Fortunately, Ms. Nicholas was right on hand and offered to put the materials aside for a day when I could come back. "You go take care of your friend," she said when I explained my abrupt departure. "History is always here."

I pondered the depth of that statement as I hurried back down the street to Mika's store. As soon as I walked in, Mika pointed to the Cozy Nook and I sat down there to wait. A few moments later, she sat down heavily in the chair across from me. She'd been busy with customers in the store and on the phone for the last hour, and we hadn't spoken at all after she texted. Now, though, I could see she was exhausted.

"You okay?" I asked.

She sighed. "Yeah, just tired. It's been busy, but sadly, people aren't buying much. I'm thinking about doing a big sale, see if I can bring in some quick cash."

I frowned. "Are things that tight?" I had thought business was really picking up for her, so I was surprised she was feeling a pinch.

She looked up at me from beneath her eyebrows and said, "I have a sort of surprise." She leaned back in the chair and held my gaze. "I'm buying the building."

"What?!" I said as I promptly put my laptop down on the table between us. "You are?"

A grin spread across her face. "I am. Remember how a few months ago I convinced my landlord to start allowing my monthly payments to build toward a down payment?"

I nodded. "I do, but I thought that was the five-year plan."

"It was. But things have been going so well that I've been able to put extra toward the payment every month." She sighed. "Now, I'm just a few thousand dollars short of the amount we agreed I needed to take over the mortgage from him."

"And you're anxious to get that taken care of?" I said as understanding dawned on me. Mika and I shared a similar impatience about achieving our goals, so I got where she was coming from.

"He's agreed that if I get him the rest of the money by the end of the month, we can execute the sale on the first." She wiggled a little in the chair. "But at this rate, I won't make it."

"All right, then let's figure out how we do this." I picked up my notebook, opened to a new page, and wrote the words *Mika's Building* at the top.

She grinned. "Okay," she said as she leaned forward.

For the next hour, between customers, Mika and I sketched a plan for her sale, a promotional event, and an extra-special push at the city market for this weekend. Her boyfriend, Chris, was already doing a bunch of marketing pushes for her in Charlottesville as part of his own food truck business, and she said he'd be happy to promote these events too. We set targets for each of the events, and when we were done with our calculations, we thought there was a good chance, if everything went really well, that she could make her payment at the end of the month.

I was so excited for her, and I loved seeing the little skip in her step as she went to help her next customer with our plan in mind. To be honest, I felt a lift in my mood, too. I had started to get an idea for how I might help Mika, assist Santiago in his investigation, and satisfy my own curiosity.

With my laptop open again, I did a new Google search for information about Millicent Cavanaugh. In the past, I'd had good luck with research that went beyond the traditional databases and research materials, and I was hoping that would be the case today.

Fortunately, "Mischievous Millie," as she was nicknamed in

the press, had been quite the legend across Virginia. Apparently, our Millie had gained a considerable reputation as a horse wrangler and was in high demand with those who raised thoroughbreds because she could, according to several articles, "tame even the wildest beast."

According to a newspaper from Richmond, Mischievous Millie was called in when the horses that pulled the canal boats along the James and Kanawha Canal, which ran from Richmond up into the Virginia mountains, got unruly. She could apparently "bring them to heel with only a few words and taps of her fingers." Another article, this one from Charlottesville, noted that "Mrs. Cavanaugh appeared to have some magical ability to sway even the wild mustangs of King Carter to her will." It seemed, however, that a woman could easily and dangerously be dubbed a witch if she was helpful to rich white men. No surprise there.

As I read the articles and began to put together Millie's life story, I began to see the story of a woman who didn't let her her misfortune stop her and put it to her advantage. From what I could tell, when her husband began to fall ill, Millie leveraged her reputation as being a bit wild and unruly and let it carve out a space for her in the business world. The more I read, the more I began to suspect that her early "thrown from a horse" incident had been more of a performance than I had believed at first, since this woman seemed to have been the original horse whisperer. The more I read, the clearer it became that she had seized an opportunity after her husband was committed, taking the rumors about her wildness and using them to her advantage. I liked her immensely.

Most of the information I could find about Millie was about her professional work, but one short editorial in the local paper from Octonia focused on her personal life and what the author called her "neglectful ways" when it came to her children. Apparently, this writer took issue with the fact that Millie was away from her teenage children for "days at a time" and speculated that the children "ran wild from dawn to dusk" without the care of their mother.

I felt myself bristle as I read that particular piece because it reeked with judgmentalism about the choices Millie made to care for her family, a judgment I had been prone to myself as a single mother from time to time. But given that sometimes even the most ugly rumor can rise up out of a shred of truth, I did a few searches on the names of Millie's children, and I found no reports that they were arrested or even implicated in anything untoward for the time.

In fact, Jemima seemed to have taken after her mother and had started a successful business herself, selling the family's surplus vegetables from a roadside stand at her home. When I did a quick newspaper search on Jemima, I found several advertisements from the later decades in her life that indicated she kept up and grew this farming business into quite the successful produce market, all managed from the small house that still stood by the road across the tracks from my garage.

Apparently, her older brothers had taken over running their father's tavern when he was committed, and while it seemed the boys had moved out and gotten married as they got older, it also seemed that even when they were teenagers they had kept their parents' minds for business. According to an 1876 article, Cavanaugh Tavern had the best ale and shepherd's pie in all the Blue Ridge.

By the time I wrapped up my research, I found myself a little emotional about the success of these two women, and the men in their lives, in a time when women were not expected or encouraged to have public personas, much less successful businesses. In more ways than I could name, they had paved the way for me and my business, and I felt even more inspired than before to keep my business growing and building a future for Sawyer.

Plus, I had a firm storyline that I could use to help promote Mika's Women of the Skein event the following weekend. She had decided to recruit the women who knitted and crocheted in her shop for a "yarn bombing" event around Octonia County. Folks would take yarn and wrap it artfully around any object they wanted, with permission of course. The goal was to raise money and awareness for an organization called Warm Up America, which took donated blanket squares and sewed them into blankets for people experiencing homelessness.

We'd decided that yarn-working women could enter a competition to acquire the most votes for their yarn bombing installation in a public space in Octonia. There were no guidelines beyond needing to have permission from the owner of the objects to be "bombed" and having the installation completed by the next Friday at midnight. Voting would take place over that whole weekend, and the yarn worker or workers with the most votes would get a $100 credit at Mika's store as well as bragging rights.

Mika would collect donations at her store, and each of the bombers was asked to include a secure donation receptacle and voting box at their location. We would ask local businesses to sell tickets for votes, and we hoped several of them would donate gift certificates for a prize to be awarded to one lucky voter.

Now, I had my story to use to promote the event as well as safely – and, without reflection on Santiago's investigation at all – dig a little deeper into the Cavanaugh family history. Millie and Jemima were going to be my features in my newsletter this weekend, and with a few carefully worded social media posts and a follow-up story before the contest ended, I figured I might learn quite a bit more about the chicken coop and maybe even about who was buried beneath it.

By the time I finished my research, it was almost time for me to go get Sawyer, but I had one last project to finish to help us promote the Women of the Skein event. I was going to yarn bomb my store canopies for the city market. I didn't crochet or knit well enough to actually stitch something on the posts, but I could wrap yarn around things without trouble. So that's what I did. By the time I left to get my son, the posts for our market canopies were colorful and bright with yarn. With the right signage, we'd get some great publicity for the event.

When I picked up Sawyer at school, his teacher walked him out to the car and said, "Can I just let you know I'm in for the yarn bombing?"

I smiled. I could never discount the speed of the Octonia gossip train. "Sure. I have your email, so I'll ask Mika to put you on her list. Any idea where you'll do it?"

She winked at me. "You'll just have to see."

Already, I could see this was going to be a fun event full of fun women. I could hardly wait for next weekend.

As usual, Saw didn't miss a beat and asked, as soon as I bent over to buckle his car seat, "What's yarn bombing, Mama?"

So on the ride home, I had to promise to help him yarn bomb his playground and his balance bike, and I figured he might as well know that we were going to yarn bomb the fence at Saul's lot, too. I just had to let Saul know first, which made me a little nervous. The man was one of the most generous people I knew, but he was also sort of a stereotypical guy. I wasn't sure how he would feel about the idea of having a bunch of yarn on his fence.

I shouldn't have worried because Saul had already heard about the event from Mika, and when I called to ask, he said he'd asked Mika to order a case of yellow yarn to match his equipment. The crew and he were already planning to spend the weekend decorating the fence. "But we're not entering, Paisley. The women on the crew agree. Since we're mostly a male outfit over here, we're just participating for camaraderie and to help collect donations. Any votes we get will go toward our favorite participant."

I laughed. "You mean Mika."

"Don't you get too sure of yourself, Missy. You never know." He clicked off the phone even more abruptly than usual, and I was left wondering what exactly Saul had up his sleeve.

As soon as I hung up with Saul and checked to be sure that the silence coming from outside meant that Sawyer was engrossed in an activity and not painting the exterior of my house with leftover concrete stain, I sat down on the porch to call Santiago and give him an update on everything.

He was a little breathless when he answered, but he still made me laugh. "Santiago's One Stop. Want a wiener or a KitKat? Both on sale."

I chuckled. "I don't think anyone has called them wieners since 1972," I said.

"You have met my mother, haven't you?" he replied as I heard the background noise on his end of the call get quieter.

"A carryover from learning English later in life?" I asked and immediately hoped that wasn't a terrible thing to say.

"Oh, you wish. No, she just likes to make me uncomfortable by using that word." He sighed. "How's your day been?"

"Eventful," I said. "Yours? It sounded like you had just sprinted a mile when you picked up the phone."

"Not a physical sprint, but I have been answering calls all day. Apparently, the bones we found were quite unusual." I heard his soft grunt as he sat down. "They were old, first off. The dating isn't certain yet, but it looks like the person lived around the turn of the twentieth century."

"Whoa, that's a long time to be buried under chickens." I tried to think through what that meant in terms of the Cavanaugh timeline but found I couldn't quite draw it all together in my head. I'd have to look at my notes.

"But that's not all. The victim was a man, as Alexandra said, but what was really interesting was that there was nothing apparent wrong with him. No visible markers for illness. No indications of injuries beyond a broken arm at one point. Nothing."

I butterflied my lips. "Hmmm. What is Alexandra thinking?"

"She's puzzled but wonders if he might have died of natural causes," Santi said.

I stared across the field below me as I tried to make sense of that idea. "Why would someone hide the bones of someone who had died naturally? That doesn't make any sense."

"Agreed, but it seems to be what the bones are telling us." He paused. "And you know what I always say."

"'Follow the evidence, not your theories.'" I smiled. We'd have this conversation a lot because his work required him to have proof first, whereas mine often required theories before I could locate the proof.

"You know me well," he said. "I was also hoping maybe you'd found some information we could use."

"And you know me if you think I might just love tracking down information. In fact, I already found some things to share. I don't know how useful it'll be to the investigation, but I did find some pretty interesting stuff." I gave him the rundown on what Jonathan Boykins had told me, and then, I filled him in on Millie and Jemima and their escapades. "Does Alexandra know how old the man was when he died?"

"Late twenties, she thinks, given that his bones didn't show signs of arthritis or anything."

I thought of Johnny, Jemima's lover, and said, "Could it have been Johnny?"

Santiago said, "Are you asking me? I have no idea. You're the historian." I could hear the smile in his voice over the line.

"Johnny was quite young when he disappeared from Jemima's life, maybe even a few decades younger than she was," I said as I worked through the theory out loud.

Santi whistled. "Go, Jemima. Talk about a cougar."

I scowled at the derogatory name that older women were given when they dated younger men. "Sheriff Shifflett, you know better."

He cleared his throat. "Sorry. Yes, I do. But she was a fierce woman, it seems, from what you tell me."

"I gather so," I said, deciding to let my fiancé's rare display of sexism slide this time. "I'm going to do some more research on her later tonight after Sawyer's asleep."

"Actually, I was wondering if I could take him out for dinner, give you an evening off?" Santi's voice was quiet, and I knew that tone. He was planning something, and he wanted my son involved.

"Sure. What are you guys going to do?" I asked without much hope of getting an answer.

As expected, Santi said, "Guy stuff. I'll have him home by seven for bedtime."

I smiled at the intrigue of his words. "See you in a couple of hours."

5

Sawyer was giddy about the idea of a night out on the town with Santi, even though it wasn't really night and we didn't live in a very big town. And when Santi pulled up in his civilian sedan at 5:30, Saw didn't even wait for him to get out of the car before he climbed into his seat in the back.

I walked over, strapped my son in, and then headed to Santi's window. He was dressed in dark jeans, a White Stripes T-shirt, and a ball cap. He looked amazing, and I had to resist the urge to suggest a change in plans so I could appreciate him. "He's a little excited," I said as I smiled toward the four-year-old bouncing behind him. "You're still not going to tell me what you're up to, are you?" I asked as I leaned over to kiss Santi.

"Nope. And Sawyer, tonight's mission is top secret," he said with a glance in the rearview mirror. "No telling anyone, not even your mama."

Sawyer looked over at me and I nodded and smiled to let him know this particular secret was okay with me. Then he put his small hand to his forehead and saluted Santi. "Aye aye, Captain," he said.

I rolled my eyes. "Get out of here, you two." I gave Santi another quick kiss and then waved as they drove back up the driveway.

Beauregard bounded toward me as I headed toward the house, and I bent down to pick him up. Typically, my large gray guy wasn't much of a cuddler, at least if it involved walking while cuddling, but tonight, he let me rub under his chin as I took a lap around the house and garden and enjoyed the song of the peepers as dusk settled in.

Back inside, Beau took a seat on one of the dining room chairs and began a rigorous bathing ritual that would later require a complete de-furring of the upholstered seat and the disposal of any number of hair balls later on. I took out a skillet, two tortillas, feta, cheddar, and black beans and made myself a rather epic quesadilla, which I ate with my fingers as I stood at the counter. It was a small luxury that wasn't afforded to me when I was trying to teach a small human table manners.

Dinner done and a glass of wine poured, I settled in at my desk with my computer. I had to make a choice about my research time again. I could delve further into Millie's life and see what else I could find, or I could gather more information about her daughter Jemima and maybe discover who this mysterious Johnny was. The choice was obvious – Johnny had already captured my imagination, and I needed to know who this man was, especially if his body had been the one tucked underneath the chicken coop at Jackie's.

I naively assumed that researching a couple named Johnny and Jemima in a small place like Octonia County, Virginia, would be easy, but it turned out to be a mite trickier than I expected, especially since everyone and their brother, not to mention their uncles, was named *John* and went by *Johnny* at the time. *Jemima* was rarer, but despite finding several mentions of Jemima and her business in the local paper, I never saw any mention of someone named Johnny, or any man for that matter.

I took another look at the census records for the decades she was alive, hoping that maybe Johnny had lived at her house for a time under the guise of being a boarder or something, but no one by that name was listed in her household.

Millie, Jemima, and all their family had been lifelong members of Lydia Baptist Church just over the hill from where we all lived, so I decided that might be a place to check. Fortunately my friend Mary, the informal but very serious historian at our own church, had recently begun to connect all the local church secretaries and historians so that they could help each other with the ever more frequent genealogical and historical research questions that were coming their way. Tonight, I hoped Mary could put me in touch with someone at Lydia.

Of course Mary did better than give me a name and number. She immediately picked up the church secretary, Tee Black, and brought her over to my house. With pie. I'd had just enough time to run the vacuum over Beauregard's dining room chair/bathtub when they arrived, and the three of us had made quick work of cutting pie, pouring tea, and starting to talk history.

After asking them to keep everything confidential, I filled both women in on the situation. Tee twirled a pearl stud in her ear as she listened and took notes, nodding along thoughtfully.

Tee Black was a member of the prominent Black family. Her dad, brother, and uncle all held various government positions in the county, and her sister ran the school PTA like it was a military regiment preparing for war. I'd never had the privilege of meeting Tee before, and while Mary had said she was the most soft-spoken member of her family, she struck me as a force herself, just without the pretense that I found in her sister. I liked her right away.

As soon as I told them all I'd found about Millie and Jemima, Tee put down her pen and said, "My two most favorite church members, those two women. Been studying them myself for a while." She bent down and pulled a huge binder out of what I had thought was just a large purse. "I believe you're looking for information on Mr. Johnny Lanford. He was quite a looker, if I do say so myself." She flipped open the binder to a colorized photo of one of the most handsome men I had ever seen.

He was what I could only describe as dapper with a low-brimmed hat over his very dark hair. The artist had given his skin a sort of olive tint, and it seemed to fit him, as if he might have a Mediterranean ancestral line. His suit was simple but well cut, and his stance made me think he would be the kind of man who casually posed for selfies in our time. He definitely wasn't lacking in confidence, but then if you looked like that, why would you be?

"Wow," I whispered as I looked at the photo.

Tee grinned. "Quite a looker, huh? This was actually a photo he had taken when he became a deacon at the church." She waggled her eyebrows. "That's saying something."

"I'll say," Mary said. "He looks like he's posing for a photo shoot." She studied the photo a bit more closely. "Is that a pistol at his hip?"

Tee leaned over toward the photo. "Well, I do believe it is. I had never noticed that, but given his line of work, it doesn't surprise me."

"What was his line of work?" I asked, hoping he was a police officer but expecting that wasn't the case.

"He was a bounty hunter, although at the time, that profession wasn't really a formal thing. Most people thought of him as a gun for hire."

"Like a mercenary?" Mary asked, her eyes wide.

"Sort of. Maybe think of it more as an ancillary for the law," Tee answered.

I thought about how short-staffed Santiago and Savannah were at the sheriff's office most of the time. The new hires, Brett and Terrace, would definitely help, but they were still going to have to bring in officers for big cases. Three people for an entire county was just too few. I could see how having a freelance law official might be helpful, even now. "What was his reputation?"

Tee smiled. "Asked like a true storyteller. He was one of the good guys. At least as far as the law was concerned. He didn't garner much favor with the men, but as far as I can tell from what I've been able to find, he wasn't quite the ladies' man people made him out to be."

I raised an eyebrow. "He and Jemima carve their initials into a tree?" I said with a smile.

"Not exactly, but they were completely devoted to each other." She grinned at me. "Want to know how I know?"

I rolled my eyes. "You have to ask?" I put my hand out with the palm up and moved my fingers back and forth toward myself. "Gimme!"

Tee laughed as she turned another page in her binder and then tapped her finger against a handwritten page in a plastic sleeve. "This here is their marriage certificate."

I gaped and reached out my hand. "The actual certificate?"

This time, Tee rolled her eyes. "Of course not. Do you think I carry around historical documents like that? This is a photocopy."

I smiled as she spun the binder to me. "So they were married."

Tee nodded.

"Were they keeping it a secret?" Mary asked before I could spit out the same question.

"It seems so. This certificate was at the church in a box of old records about baptisms and weddings. But most of those were just church notes or programs. This is the legal certificate, the only one I've ever seen in our files. I am assuming the pastor didn't file it with the county for a particular reason."

I stared hard at the certificate. It was exactly the same as the dozens I'd studied at the clerk's office except that it didn't have the official mark of the clerk. "Could it have just been an oversight on the pastor's part?"

Tee shrugged. "Could have been, I guess, but something tells me that maybe they didn't want folks to know they were married."

"Because of the age difference?" I asked as I studied the dates on the certificate. Johnny was a full thirty-four years younger than his wife, and they'd gotten married when he was just twenty and she was fifty-four. Even now that would draw some attention.

"I have no earthly idea, Paisley. Seems as good a possibility as any," Tee said.

I studied the certificate a bit longer, but I wasn't going to get any more information about their stories from that piece of paper, as incredible as it was. "What else have you got in this magical binder of yours, Tee?" I said with a smile.

The woman's face broke open like I'd just asked her to show me pictures of her children or grandchildren, and she flipped to the front. "I thought you'd never ask."

So began a wonderful hour of history that took us through the Cavanaughs' lifetimes and through a story of immigration and survival in a time when both were often deadly. But it was really when we got to Millie's story that I perked up, especially when Tee said, "If I could be any person in history, I would be Millie Cavanaugh."

As she flipped the next page of her binder, I gasped. There, in a sepia-toned photo, was Millie herself, a floppy hat, leather skirt, and boots that looked like they could both kick tail and haul it, too. Her expression looked halfway between a laugh and a scowl, and yet, somehow I thought it was her typical look. I loved her even more now, and I could certainly see why Tee admired her so much.

"Tell me more," Mary said as she leaned down and ran a finger along Millie's skirt in the photo. "She looks tough as nails."

"She was," Tee said. "Could tame a wild stallion in less than five minutes, the legend says." She tapped the picture with her pointer finger. "But I'm not much of a horse person. It's how she let the horses help her and others that I love."

I leaned closer. "What do you mean she let the horses help her?" I had visions of her running whiskey or maybe being a part of the Underground Railroad. Either sounded amazing to me.

Tee winked at me. "I think you'll like this," she said. "She and Jemima helped women escape abusive situations."

Mary sat back and whistled. "Whoa."

"Whoa is right," Tee said. "It was incredibly dangerous for her and her charges, but from the two accounts I've read of women who Millie helped escape, she had a really careful process."

"I need to read those accounts," I said.

"I thought you might want them." She slid two pieces of paper over to me. "I made you some copies."

I started to read, but the handwriting was faint and very scrawling, like the notes had been written in haste. "Can you tell us a bit so I can spare my eyesight?" I asked Tee.

"Definitely. First, you should know that Millie seems to have taken a lot of her practices from the Underground Railroad, including the fact that she asked women to recount their stories for her book. Unfortunately, that book doesn't survive, it seems. I found these two fragments in Millie's papers that she donated to the church for safekeeping near the end of her life. But the book itself, it's disappeared."

I groaned. That was a huge loss to history, that.

Tee nodded. "I feel the same way, but here's what I've gleaned from what Millie said herself. She'd get word about a woman in need through one of her kids or Johnny. He worked, sometimes, at one of the tanneries in town and made a point of taking his lunch break alone and out at the edge of the woods so that women who needed to get Millie a message could talk to him from the cover of the trees."

"A man putting himself in harm's way for women. I like Johnny," Mary said, expressing exactly what I felt. I could see Santiago doing that, and I couldn't wait to tell him about Johnny.

"Sometimes people left notes at Jemima's vegetable stand, too, apparently, and when Jemima was old enough, she helped Millie on the runs, too." Tee turned a page. "As best I can tell, this is a list of people in Charlottesville that would take women and their kids in and help them get a new start."

I scanned the list of last names and numbers. "No street names? Just in case?" I asked.

"I'm thinking so. Charlottesville was pretty small then, so I expect Millie just needed a little mnemonic to help her remember."

On the next page of the book, I saw a photo of a woman and three teenage children. "This is Annabelle Harris. She grew up in Octonia. When her husband started hitting her and her girls, her son" – Tee pointed to a wiry boy with a shock of blond hair in the middle of the picture – "her son Emmett tried to stop him. Almost died. That's when Annabelle decided to run."

I glanced back at the handwritten pages before me. "Is one of these stories hers?" I asked.

Tee nodded. "Yep, and Millie had this photo in her papers

with their names written on the back." She flipped the page, and I saw the name *Avery Humboldt* written there.

"She changed her name. Of course she did." I shook my head. The lengths these women had gone to protect themselves in a time when the law didn't even pretend to do so. "Millie kept in touch with the women?"

"Yep. Apparently, they gathered once a year or so at a secret location and caught up. A sort of survivors' support group and networking event all in one. Long after Millie died, Jemima kept them going." She flipped the page and there was a newspaper article about the "Survivor's Club." The article was dated 1898.

"Whoa," Mary said as she scanned the article. "That's incredible." She sat back. "I wonder if any of these women's descendants know about Millie or the group she and her daughter ran?"

Tee closed her binder. "That I can't tell you, but it's worth a little query, huh?" She winked at me and stood up. "I best get going. Those bulletins don't print themselves." She walked toward the door. "Mary, want a ride back?"

Mary looked at me. "Please."

I hugged her and then went to hug Tee and thank her again. "I'll keep you posted on what we find."

"Please do, and if you need anything else, you know where I am." She walked out the door and to her red Fiat convertible. I laughed. Millie and Jemima weren't the only spitfires of Octonia, apparently.

"Catch up with you in the morning. Coffee and donuts here at 8:30?" Mary asked as she followed Tee out the door.

"You know the way right to my heart."

THE NEXT MORNING, Sawyer woke up early, much to my chagrin. After cajoling him into eating a waffle, get dressed, and actually climbing into the car, I had already finished my first pot of coffee. I needed to make a fresh pot of coffee for Mary and me when she arrived. "Well, isn't Tee just something?" I said as I sat down beside her.

"She is, but I thought about Millie and Jemima all night. Those women were incredible," Mary said. "What are we going to look into first? Millie or the group she started?"

This is why I loved my friends. They were totally on board with my work and had adopted it as their own. "Let's do both. Maybe we can hit town and look into this group Millie started, and then maybe ask Tee if we can look at Millie's papers at the church?"

"Sounds good," Mary said. "Any excuse to go to town and visit Wegmans." The big grocery store in Charlottesville was a treat for most of us that lived a distance away. Mary, Mika, and I had started taking girls' night dates there from time to time so we could enjoy the hot food, pick up some special chocolate, and get our grocery shopping done all at the same time.

"Lucky," I said. "Remind me to get some naan while we're there?" I could eat that stuff by the pound.

"Of course," she said. "Want to go today? I'm off work."

I looked at my friend and wondered if she had specifically taken a vacation day to help me with this research. If she had, God love her for it.

"It's a bit early to hit the archives, right?" she asked. When I nodded, she said, "For now, what do we look at?" She flipped open her laptop and opened a tab for her browser. "I can take newspapers if you want."

"Perfect," I said. "I'm going to delve into some of the finding aids at UVA and see if I can get any more information to complement what Tee brought."

Soon, both of us were tapping away at our computers, and I smiled because it felt like college again, where my roommates and I were up late at night finishing papers for the next day.

Except, of course, Mary and I were solidly in middle age and would not stay up all night willingly, even for research.

The collections at UVA were not revealing much at all, which sadly didn't surprise me. Unless you were a very wealthy woman who was, in all likelihood, married to a rich and prominent man, it wasn't likely you'd show up beyond a mention in historical documents altogether, much less in the overarching outline available in most finding aids.

I was about to give up when I decided to search for Avery Humboldt's name. Given that she'd had the means to have a professional portrait of herself and her children taken, I thought it was possible she might show up in documents, too. Sure enough, some of her letters were preserved in a collection at the library. "Looks like we have our first hit at the Special Collections Library. Want to dig in with me?"

"Do I get to share your naan?" Mary asked.

I let out a hard sigh. "I suppose," I said with a grin. "You find anything?"

"A couple of articles where Millie's arrest is mentioned, which is interesting but not very telling." She shook her head. "Well, not very telling about her, but it speaks volumes about the times."

I couldn't disagree with that. "Feel like heading into town for an early lunch? I mean, if you think you can find something on Millie's women there?"

"That's exactly what I was thinking," she said as she bumped her elbow against mine. "Wegmans for lunch and then research."

"Yes, girl," I said, channeling some sort of sassy teenager I never was. "I'm going to ask Mika if she can come, too." I knew she was busy with the store and her yarn bombing project, but I also knew she'd be sad if she thought we didn't want her along.

My text to my best friend brought back a resounding *yes* because, apparently, she had some things she needed for the store and because she really wanted lunch too. I told her we'd pick her up in a half hour.

As Mary continued to research, I checked in with Claire to be sure everything was going okay at my store. Since I'd brought her on, I'd been able to give myself more time for research and actual salvage projects, and now that she was taking night classes in history, she had asked if she could get more hours and work on her schoolwork at the shop. I loved that combination and was thrilled she found working with old things as interesting as I did. Plus she was really good with sales – better than I was, honestly, because she wasn't nervous about pressuring people to buy. Since she'd gone full-time, my sales numbers had gone up by 20 percent.

"All good, Ms. Paisley," Claire said when I called. "Just sold that large metal gate we had hanging in the front office. Anything you want me to put there in its place?"

I was a little sad to hear the gate had sold, but when I realized it had been priced at a premium simply because I had loved it so much, I didn't complain. "Use your best judgment," I said. "It's what I look at when I'm there, so pick something I like."

She laughed. "So not the taxidermized goose?" Claire teased.

"Please no." I'd picked up a taxidermy collection from a local estate sale because those creepy creatures were really popular with some folks. But I had staged them upstairs in one of the rooms because I couldn't stand looking at their little faces. "Not unless you want to give me nightmares."

Claire laughed. "No need for that. I'll find something less creepy."

I smiled and hung up. Mary had already packed our laptop bags, poured two to-go mugs of coffee, and was waiting by the door for me. "Ready?"

"As I'll ever be," I said as I took my bag and coffee and followed her out the door.

When we got to Mika's shop, she was waiting outside for us, her own mug of coffee in hand. "I feel like I'm skipping school," she said as she climbed into my back seat.

"Great," Mary said. "Let's go be wild and reckless like we were when we were teenagers."

I caught Mika's eye in the rearview mirror and then looked over at Mary. The three of us started laughing at the same moment. "Did either of you two skip school?" she asked when she stopped laughing. "I never did, so I don't know why I think this is what that feels like."

"Nope, not once. That would have been far too reckless for me," I said with another giggle.

"My mother would have beat my tail if I'd ever played hooky. I was too scared," Mary added.

"Well, then we'll just have to pretend. What would three teenagers do if they skipped school?" Mika asked. "Get piercings or tattoos?"

I chuckled. "I'm not thinking that out here in the country those were the top pastimes. I'm thinking more smoking and drinking."

Mary nodded. "I'm not up for smoking, but I could be convinced to get a midday cocktail."

"Me, too," Mika added.

"Then that's what we'll do. Wegmans, research, dollar store, and then a cocktail," I said. "And I don't even have a curfew today."

"Sawyer is going to his grandparents?" Mika asked.

"His dad is taking him camping, so he's picking him up from school today." I spun my hair around my finger and pretended to snap bubble gum. "We can be as wild as we want."

Mika rolled her window down and stuck her head out into the open air. "Yahoo!" she shouted.

Mary looked at her when she came back in. "How did it feel?"

"Amazing. Give it a try."

Mary smiled and said, "Don't mind if I do." She rolled down her window, and then both she and Mika had their heads out the windows and were screaming at the top of their lungs.

I put on my sunglasses and hoped we weren't passing anyone I knew. And then I smiled and turned up the '80s station.

THE THREE OF us gorged ourselves on fried foods at the hot food bars around Wegmans and then bought far too much junk and absolutely no produce before heading over to the library. The rules around access to the materials at the library were pretty strict, so I warned my two friends that we were going to have to rein it in for a couple of hours while we worked. From the snickers the two of them exchanged, I wondered if that was going to be possible, but when we arrived, they took deep breaths, filled out the paperwork to register as guests, and quickly delved into research – Mary on Millie's group of women and Mika on Johnny Lanford.

I delved further into Avery Humboldt's story by asking for two boxes that contained her letters. Soon enough, all three of us were settled at the research tables with green boxes of materials before us.

It was a Friday afternoon, so there weren't any student researchers on hand – sunny day, weekend ahead. But one man who looked about our age was tucked into a corner with his computer and his own box of materials. Between his presence and the careful eye of the archivists beyond the glass research-room wall, we managed to keep our silliness in check while we worked.

Soon enough, I lost myself in the files before me and in Avery Humboldt's story as I could piece it together from the letters her friends wrote her. The earliest note was dated 1860 and was from a woman named Beth who lived in Octonia town. Beth's letter was breezy and full of news about the goings-on, including the county fair and the latest engagement announcements and births.

I enjoyed the letter because it was about my home, but it was the last line that really caught my attention. "'You may have heard that Hen Harris has taken himself a new bride. I hope to be in touch with her soon to welcome her to the community.'"

My laptop was already logged into the genealogy site, and I quickly did a search in 1860 for "Hen Harris" in Octonia. Sure enough, he was listed there with his wife, Cynthia. The girl was only sixteen. I felt my heart quicken.

The 1850 census showed Hen Harris living with his wife Annabelle and their three children, of whom Emmett was the oldest. So this was definitely Annabelle's husband, and I couldn't help but think that Beth was giving Avery an update on her ex. I wondered what that would mean, and exactly what Beth knew.

I didn't have to wait long to find out because in Beth's next letter, dated just two months later, she had the same breezy style but also mentioned that she did indeed call on Mrs. Cynthia Harris and that the poor woman seemed to have taken a bad fall recently.

I felt understanding pass through my body like an electrical surge. Beth was letting Avery know that her husband was beating his new wife. I couldn't help but think that maybe Beth was part of Millie's secret network to help women get out.

Mika and Mary leaned close while I explained what I found, and then Mary said, "Look at this." She pointed to a headline on her screen that said, *Octonia Man Found Dead Outside His Own Home.*

I scanned the article and saw that the body had been discovered by the man's wife one Sunday morning before church. He'd been shot. I flitted my eyes through the words looking for names – apparently, it was the murder that was the big news, not the identity of the victim – and finally found what I was looking for – Hen Harris. He had been the victim.

I sat back hard in my chair as Mika let out a soft whistle. "Holy cow," she whispered. "That can't be a coincidence, can it?"

"What's the date on the article?" I asked Mary.

"October 1860," she said.

I shook my head. "No coincidence at all. Someone killed Hen Harris, and I'd be willing to bet money it was because he was beating yet another woman."

"You think Millie and her group took the law into their own hands?" Mary asked.

I shrugged. "I don't know who did the killing, but I bet we've just found what Millie and her group did when they couldn't help the woman get away."

Mika's eyes went wide. "You really think so?"

"I have no proof, but yeah, I do." I looked at Mary. "What led you to this article?"

Mary nodded and slid a piece of paper over to me. At the top she'd written, *Women linked to Millie Cavanaugh*. Below, she had a list of six names. "These were all the women mentioned in articles related to Millie. All of them had brought Millie in to help them tame a wild horse."

"Would women have done that?" Mika said. "Seems like something a man of the time would do. Could women even own horses?"

"I have the same questions, but somehow, some way, Millie

got herself into close proximity to these women." Mary tapped the screen. "We just have to figure out how."

I let out a long puff of air. "Let's keep looking, see what we find," I said.

At that moment, the man who had been working in the corner stepped to our table. I expected him to ask us to keep it down so he could do his work, but instead, he stretched out his hand and said, "I'm Josh Lanford. Forgive me for interrupting. I think, though, we may be researching the same story. My great-great-grandfather was Johnny Lanford."

6

I stared at the man for a very long time before Mary prodded me in the back to wake me out of my shocked stupor. "Sorry. Nice to meet you." I introduced myself, Mary, and Mika, and then told him we were actually researching Millie Cavanaugh, a sort of test to see if he knew what we were talking about. I felt a little uneasy, given the nature of this research, revealing Millie's work to any man. It was silly, I knew, but also a simple result of having hard enough troubles with men in my life to be a little leery of trusting them with any women's stories.

"Wow. Johnny's mother-in-law. She was amazing," Josh said with a grin. "Are you looking into her network to help women escape their husbands?"

For another long moment, I stared at the man above me, but finally I said, "We are, and I would like to know everything you know."

"Awesome. I have to finish up just this last bit of research, but if you want, we could all go sit outside and enjoy the sun while we swap stories." He looked around. "No one else is here now, though, if you feel more comfortable staying here."

I looked at my friends, and Mika smiled. "Let's finish up and hit the Lawn. I haven't sunbathed on a warm fall afternoon in a couple of decades."

"Sounds like a plan," Mary added.

All four of us then went back to our boxes, and I scanned the rest of Beth's letters to Avery. Beth never said anything direct, and for good reason, but when I reached her letter of late October 1860, she said that Hen Harris had been tragically shot outside his house. "The killer is unknown, but Ms. Cavanaugh has assured the authorities that she saw two strange men on horses near the Harris house that night."

I snickered. "Good on you, Millie," I whispered.

Quickly, I scanned the rest of the letters and looked for any other correspondence from Octonia. Not finding any, I made note of the other women's names on the letters and then returned the box to the archivists. Mary and Mika followed suit soon after, and then Josh Lanford handed his back, asking the staff to hold it for him until Monday. The four of us then grabbed our things and headed up from the underground archives into the sunlight of a fall afternoon in Virginia.

I had a picnic blanket in my car for such instances when Saw and I decided to take advantage of good weather, but given that we'd parked fifteen minutes off campus to save a few dollars, I wasn't about to walk that far. Fortunately, there was an empty picnic table just across from the Old Hospital, and the four of us sat down and reintroduced ourselves without feeling the need to whisper.

"I'm so sorry to have been eavesdropping," Josh said, "but when I heard you say Octonia and the name Millie, I couldn't help myself. She's a long-lost treasure of Virginia."

"So right," Mary said. "She was amazing." She leaned back and put her face to the sun before looking at Josh and saying, "But tell us about Johnny. He's kind of a mystery."

A smile broke across Josh's face, and I realized that he was even younger than I had imagined, maybe just in his early 30s. His serious expression in the archives had led me to believe him quite a bit older.

"Well, I'll tell you what I know, but stop me if I'm just sharing information you already have." He looked at the three of us and then said, "He was a gunslinger who covered his tracks by working at the tannery. That's probably the short description."

I laughed. "If you're writing a book, that's what I'd use in the description."

"I am writing a book, actually, and I should jot that down, I guess." He took out a piece of paper and made a quick note before looking back up at us. "Unfortunately, that's the only really concrete information I have so far. There are lots of stories about how he helped his mother-in-law." He stopped for a moment. "Well, I think Millie was his mother-in-law, of a sort. I can't find any record that he and her daughter Jemima ever married, though."

Now, it was my turn to grin. "Oh, they were married." I took the copy of Jemima and Johnny's marriage certificate out of my bag. "See?"

"What?!" Josh shouted as he scanned the page. "Where did you get this?"

I explained about Tee Black and the church records, about how we weren't sure why the certificate had never been filed.

"Can I take a picture of this?" Josh asked as he held up his phone.

"Just keep that copy. I can ask Tee for another one," I said as something dawned on me. "Is Jemima your great-grandmother?"

Josh smiled again. "Sure is. I didn't get her or Grandma Millie's spunk, but I can grow a good zucchini."

Mika, Mary, and I laughed. "Green thumbs are genetic, huh?" Mika said. "Good to know."

I studied Josh a minute. He had the same dark hair as his great-great-grandfather Johnny but his complexion was much fairer, at least if the colorized photo of Johnny had been accurate. He was also a bit heavier set than his ancestor, who had looked like he could have used a bit more food, to be honest. "Forgive me for asking, but was your great-grandfather—" I interrupted myself. "I'm assuming it was a great-grandfather, since you still have the name Lanford."

Josh nodded. "Right, Grandpa Joe."

I smiled. "You're all *J* names?"

"Johnny, Joe, Jeb, Julius, Jonas, and Josh." He nodded.

"Okay, so Joe? That was Johnny's son," I asked. When Josh nodded again, I said, "Again, forgive me, but was he born in secret?"

Josh's face grew more serious. "Yeah. Jemima went to Charlottesville to have Joe. I always thought that was because they weren't legally married, but I guess I'm going to have to rethink that."

I looked out across the grassy field full of students in various states of nap, studying, or talking and sighed. "I hear ya," I said. "But I'm thinking it might have been for another reason. What year was your Grandpa Joe born?"

Josh glanced down at the notebook on the table in front of him and flipped back a few pages. "1897." His eyes skipped over to the marriage certificate I had just shown him. "They weren't married yet." He looked up at me.

"So you were right, but also, Jemima was fifty-two years old. I'm guessing she came down here to give birth in a hospital just in case there were complications." I looked across the road to the red brick building that, suddenly, seemed far more important than it had ten minutes earlier. I pointed to the hospital. "That was the only hospital in Charlottesville at the time."

For a few moments, all of us stared at the building where Josh's great-grandfather had been born. I took a deep breath and exhaled a thank-you for not just one but two amazing feats of contact today. First Josh, and now the hospital right next to us.

Mary let out a long, slow groan. "Fifty-two years old back then was quite old."

"Tell me about it. I had Saw when I was forty-three, and it was brutal. I mean, Jemima was probably in great shape, given all her gardening, but still." I winced at the very thought of her recovery and resisted the urge to ask Josh whether she'd needed a C-section. I could probably look that up myself and spare the man the image of his grandmother giving birth.

Josh was simply staring at the hospital building, and I knew well the feeling of overwhelm that was etched over his face. I'd seen it in my own reflection any number of times when the trajectories of research had left me dumbfounded. I was actually pretty close to that state today, myself.

"Hey, give me your number. I'll text you so you'll have mine. Then, we can keep in touch about research," I said as I tapped him on the arm, breaking his gaze at the hospital.

He nodded and slowly said his number as I tapped it into my phone and then sent him a quick text. "And if you ever want to dig around in Octonia, come on up. We can show you around." I gestured to the two women beside me. "It would be our pleasure."

"It would," Mika said, "and next weekend, we're having an event for my store, and we'll be honoring Millie and Jemima there. We'd love to have you there to accept a small token of our thanks for their inspiration."

Josh nodded. "I'll be there. And thanks." He stood up and gave us a little wave as he walked slowly toward The Corner, the section of shops just off Grounds at UVA. The poor guy was just dumbstruck. It would take him a bit to process all he'd just learned about his family, so I set a reminder to send him a text on Sunday to remind him about Mika's event.

I turned to her. “So you’re going to honor Millie and Jemima on Saturday?” I hadn’t yet told her about my plans to feature them in my newsletter, but I chalked this up to the third big alignment of goodness for the day.

“Yeah,” Mika said. “Seems like the perfect choice, and a great way to learn more about their history.”

“And maybe get a clue about who was buried under their chicken coop,” Mary added.

“Exactly why I’m writing about them in my newsletter this week, so I can really plug the event this weekend, too.” I stood up and stretched. “Tell us about what Chris is doing for promo while we walk to the car?”

As we strolled back across Grounds to my car, Mika shared about the flyers Chris had made to distribute at the truck, about the yarn bombing his daughter had done on the bistro tables they put out wherever they set up, and about how he’d revised his website to advertise 10 percent off if people mentioned the Women of the Skein event in Octonia. “I’m impressed,” Mary said as we got into my car. “Want me to announce it at church on Sunday?”

Mika raised her eyebrows. “That would be appropriate?”

“Of course,” Mary said. “Not everything has to be churchy to be spiritual. And our folks would love to support a local business and learn about the women of our history.”

“That would be awesome. Maybe some women would want to yarn bomb something at the church,” I said.

“No maybe about it. Just wait until you see our display.” Mary grinned and shrugged in what, I thought, was supposed to be an innocent manner but actually made her look a bit more like Sawyer did when he stole an extra piece of chocolate.

“This is going to be amazing,” I said as we headed out of downtown. “But we really need to talk about our cocktail plans. I vote on somewhere with tequila and tortilla chips.”

“Yes, woman,” Mary said.

A few minutes later, we pulled into the Mexican place just north of town and then spent the next two hours slowly sipping our margaritas, eating all the nachos deluxe we could, and laughing about our far-too-uptight teenage selves. It was a perfect afternoon, and when I dropped off Mika and Mary, they were both laughing so hard that they had tears in their eyes. Apparently the story about the time I fell in the manhole next to the highway with my skirt over my head was especially funny after the second margarita they'd both enjoyed because I was driving.

I WAS FEELING amazing when I pulled into my driveway, and my delight continued when Santiago met me with a fresh margarita and suggested we take to the porch. For a few minutes, we just sat and enjoyed the fall-scented evening. The leaves hadn't yet begun to drop yet, but I swore I could smell them in the air. Or maybe it was the small bonfire Santiago had lit.

After a while, he said, "So tell me about the research trip?"

I had texted him when we left to ask if he'd learned anything else that might be helpful in my research, but he didn't have anything to add because Alexandra hadn't found anything else about the body.

I filled him in on what we'd discovered in the documents, and then I told him all about Josh Lanford. "A secret child? Can you believe it?"

Santiago just stared at me for a minute, and then he put down his drink. "I can't believe it, actually," he said. "Jemima didn't have any children."

I shook my head. "No, she didn't have any children here, but she gave birth in Charlottesville. That's what Josh said."

"No, she didn't, Pais. Alexandra pulled her medical records because she wanted to see if maybe she'd had a boy at some point." He looked at me carefully. "She had a hysterectomy when she was thirty-two, and she'd never given birth."

I stared at him. "Say that again?"

"She had her uterus removed when she was thirty-two years old. The medical records indicated that she had never had children. Alexandra thinks she probably had uterine cancer and that she maybe couldn't have children because of that." Santiago took my hand. "Sorry. This looks like you're taking it hard."

I took a long, deep breath and checked in with myself because Santi was right. Tears had come to my eyes, and I wasn't sure why. I sat back and closed my eyes. That's when I felt it, the grief of having battled infertility myself, the grief for Jemima who I thought had maybe won that battle so late in life but apparently hadn't. I was so sad for her.

But then, I had to remind myself that she may have not wanted children, that I couldn't superimpose my experience on hers. Still, though, a hysterectomy at thirty-two, that was a big surgery, especially then, and a big part of yourself to lose so early in life.

Santiago rocked in his chair for a few minutes, giving me the quiet I needed to digest this big news. Then he looked over and said, "Want to talk about that?"

I shook my head. Santi knew how hard it had been for me to have Sawyer, and I was sure he had put two and two together. Sometime, we'd circle back to this moment and talk about it, but for now, my mind had moved on. "So why would Josh Lanford lie about that?"

Santiago shrugged. "Maybe he's not lying. Maybe there's a mistake in the records?"

"Only one way to find out," I said and stood up. "Care to be my stenographer again?"

"Always, but first, more margaritas." He took our glasses

and led the way to the door. "I also have fajita makings all ready for later."

I leaned over and said, "Have I told you lately that I love you?"

"You haven't, but I'd prefer if you sing it instead," he said with a twinkle in his eye.

I bumped my hip against his, and he said, "Watch it. I might spill this tiny bit of margarita, and that would be a waste."

It didn't take long for me to cue up the UVA hospital records on my laptop. Since the archivists had prioritized digitizing them, I found – quite easily – that what Josh had told me was accurate. A woman named Jemima Lanford had given birth to a baby boy at the hospital on June 9, 1897. The father was listed as Jonathan Lanford, and a few clicks through the genealogy site confirmed the exact lineage of men with 'J' names that Josh had given me.

As Santiago wrote down what I found, I sipped my margarita and breathed a sigh of relief. I had really liked Josh, and while I knew that people I liked sometimes got things wrong or purposefully deceived others, I was very glad to find that this hadn't been the case here.

The situation did, however, bring up another huge mystery: who was this Jemima Lanford?

"Is there any chance that Alex found the wrong person?" I asked Santiago in the kitchen a few minutes later as we prepared the fajitas for dinner.

"That's what I'm wondering, too." He handed me the spatula so I could keep stirring the peppers, onions, and mushrooms. "Let me text her."

"Invite her over," I said. "We have plenty, and it might help for the three of us to talk this out."

"Good idea," he said as he picked up his phone.

One of the things that Alexandra and I had connected over was the fact that she was a single mom whose child's dad took him on the weekends. For both of us, that meant our weeks were often very, very full, but it also meant our weekends were more open than those of other parents. We'd taken to the farmers' market in town several times and enjoyed the fact that we, unlike many of the other parents there, didn't have to keep saying "don't poke the fresh bread" or "I don't think you're going to like blue cheese" when the child took a free sample and then promptly spit it out in front of the maker.

Tonight, when she came over, she was in yoga pants, a workout tank, and a headband. "Don't let the outfit fool you," she said as she came in with a peanut butter pie from the Mennonite market up the road. "This is how I Friday, and it doesn't include any sort of exercise."

I laughed. "If it doubles as pajamas for the night, we might be twins."

"Ooh, I hadn't thought of that, but I may just try it." She took the margarita that Santi handed her and said, "Thank you so much. I would have been bingeing junk food something awful if you hadn't invited me over."

"Bingeing has its important place," Santi said as he took over the cooking and gestured for the two of us to sit. "But we're glad you're here all the same."

As the two of us sat down, and I admired the handsome man moving around the kitchen with aplomb, Alexandra and I exchanged the various information we'd gathered from our search, and very quickly, we could see we were very definitely talking about different women. My Jemima *Lanford* was fifty-two years old when she gave birth to Joe. Alexandra's Jemima *Cavanaugh* was thirty-two when she had a full hysterectomy, meaning there was no way she could carry a child.

"By today's medical standard, it would have been unlikely to recommend a full hysterectomy except in the case of very severe and advanced cancer. Jemima was just so young," Alexandra said.

"But back then …" I left the statement unfinished because I knew that Alexandra had studied medical history as an undergrad. She knew that women were often subjected to far more invasive surgeries than would be deemed necessary now because doctors didn't really bother to understand female anatomy.

Alexandra nodded. "If it's okay with you, maybe we can not think about that."

I touched my friend's hand briefly and then changed the subject. "So do we think it a coincidence that the woman in Charlottesville is named Jemima Lanford?"

Santiago sighed. "No such thing as coincidences. That woman took the Jemima from up here's name."

He sounded so sure, and I felt pretty sure myself. But I also knew we had to find some evidence of that or the sheriff wouldn't be satisfied. "So how do we prove that?"

"Do we need to prove it?" Alexandra asked.

Santi brought us each a plate of tortillas and then carried over a platter of peppers, onions, and mushrooms. "It's all related to the Cavanaughs somehow, and we do have a murder to solve?" he said.

"Do we know it was a murder?" Alexandra asked as she piled veggies on her first tortilla. "I haven't seen any evidence of murder."

"Are you just trying to play devil's advocate?" Santi asked, and I could hear a little frustration in his voice.

She looked at him closely. "No." She shook her head. "Sorry. No, I'm really not. My role is to determine cause of death, and so far, everything points to the fact that this man died of natural causes."

I sighed. "Okay, so let's say we use that as our hypothesis. Why would someone bury him under a chicken coop?"

"That, Pais, is really the question, and I don't think it's one that medical science or police investigation is going to give us an answer to," Santi said before taking a huge bite of his fajita.

I raised one finger into the air and hoisted my hand over my head. "This is a case for history," I said in my best movie announcer voice.

Everyone cracked up, and the tension of a moment before dissipated completely. "Who feels like a good old research session?"

Alexandra looked at Santi and over at me. "I have never heard someone so excited about the prospect of research," she said with a smile. "But sure, count me in."

"You're off tomorrow, right?" I asked my fiancé.

He looked at me out of the corner of his eye and said a slow, "Yes. Why?"

"What do you say to a research, yarn bombing, cookout combo at my shop?" I winked as if I'd just suggested we all head to Vegas for a weekend of unencumbered fun instead of a lot of work with old papers and computers.

"Sounds fun ... ish?" Alexandra said with a smirk. "I'm in. What can I bring?"

I looked over at the pie she'd brought along. "Can you get a couple more of those?" I patted my stomach. "I don't think I can eat another bite."

She laughed. "Sure."

"I'll get the cookout supplies and talk to Saul about using his cooker." Saul had recently created his own pig cooker out of an old oil barrel. At first, I had thought the idea entirely gross, but he'd cleaned the barrel really well and the scent of slowly cooking pork had wooed me. It was the best BBQ I'd ever eaten.

"Ooh, yes, and see if he and his crew are planning to do their yarn bombing tomorrow. We can invite them, too." I was getting excited.

Santiago laughed and pretended to write on his hand. "Get

food for five thousand. Think we can count on a small boy with loaves and fishes?"

I rolled my eyes. "Let me reach out to Ms. Nicholas and see what, if any, materials she's comfortable bringing over for us to look at. Alexandra, do you mind reaching out to Mary and Mika, see if they want to come?"

"On it," she said as she picked up her phone.

Claire would be at the Charlottesville market tomorrow, so I could work and research at the same time. I hoped Mrs. Stephenson was able to cover for Mika at the store and that she'd feel comfortable stepping away for a few hours.

"Savannah's in, too," Santi said as he began to load the dishwasher. "Brett can handle things and call us if he needs us. It'll be a good opportunity for him to learn the ropes with a safety net nearby."

"Awesome. Now, I need to start organizing information so that everyone has something to do." First thing, I texted Ms. Nicholas and explained my plan. She said she'd be happy to bring over everything about the Cavanaughs and Lanfords – *I just found a bit of a treasure trove about Johnny's family*, she said – and help us dig through it.

With those documents on hand, I just needed to make a list of what online sources we had and what, if anything, we'd need to go to the clerk's office for later since they weren't open on Saturdays. For a brief minute, I thought about calling the clerk, Trissy, an old high school friend, to see if she could open up just for us, but then I realized that was a big ask and one I might need to make at a time when I was certain there was information to be had ... and when we weren't still trying to keep a mysterious body under wraps.

Which reminded me. "Santi, are there historical police records somewhere?"

He shook his head. "Not really. I'm not sure that back in the day anyone kept formal records." He tapped a finger against his cheek, just like Sawyer does, making me wonder which of them had passed on the habit. "However, Savannah has been cleaning out the back room and found a couple of boxes of old documents—"

I interrupted him. "Old documents, and I'm just hearing about them now?" I said with mock dismay.

He rolled his eyes. "Let me ask her if she can bring them along tomorrow. It may be nothing, but it'll be a chance to sort through them at least."

I smiled. "I like that plan."

By the time Alex left an hour later, we knew that Saul and his crew were in fact decorating their fence, and he had suggested I figure out something on the house that served as our office to decorate, too. The cooker was on site, and Santi was ready with a shopping list that Saul had insisted on covering the costs for. Mika, Mary, Savannah, Dad, and Lucille were all planning to come, and Ms. Nicholas was bringing along at least four boxes of material for us to look through, "away from any beverages," as she stressed. It was going to be a good research day.

Santi and I took hot tea to the porch after I'd finished my notes about what materials we needed to check, and while the cool air of the autumn evening blew through, we held hands and rocked. I had an image of us as an old couple, sitting in the same spot doing the same thing, and I settled into the peace of that idea.

7

The next morning, I was awake before the sun, all invigorated for our group research session. I was a little nervous about how I was going to keep everyone organized, but after a few minutes of meditating on the fact that I had all I needed to do this project and that everyone coming was someone I loved and trusted, I let the nerves go and started to just lean into the excitement.

I'd asked everyone who could to bring their laptops, and I felt fairly sure we would have enough computers for what we needed to do. I had gathered up all the spare notebooks I had from around the house and cleared out any used pages full of toddler scribbles or my random research notes. Someday I was going to have to get all those organized, but not today.

Today, I had a mystery – actually several mysteries – to solve, but first, coffee. Santiago had already set up the French press and the kettle the night before, so I put the water on to boil and sat down with my notes. I'd gotten a late-night text from Mary saying that Tee Black had expressed interest in coming with the church records, and I'd responded with a *yes* and about a thousand exclamation points.

As I waited for the coffee to be ready, I added the church records to my list of resources and began tentatively assigning people to tasks. I wasn't going to be a stickler about my assignments, but I figured it would help if I could suggest points of focus for people.

When Santiago came out a few minutes later, smelling all good like soap and aftershave, I had everything organized and a solid plan for our day ahead. He kissed my cheek and said, "You were up early."

"I'm so excited," I said as I stood and stamped my feet a little for emphasis. I poured us both a cup of coffee and then walked him through my research plans. "You and Savannah, of course, will look at the police records, but then I thought Lucille could work with Tee."

"Oh, they'll enjoy each other," Santi said as he sipped his coffee. I had told him about how much I'd liked Tee, and I thought the same thing – she and Lucille would be fast friends.

Since Dad wasn't much for sitting still, I thought maybe he could help Saul and crew with the yarn bombing on the fence and then on the posts of our front porch. Of course, then, he could help staff the cooker with Santi later in the afternoon.

Mika and Mary were already well familiar with the online records, so I thought I'd pass those along to them. Then, Alexandra and I would work with Ms. Nicholas on what she was bringing from the historical society. I hoped that would make her feel a bit less nervous about having those precious files out of their building since I knew how to handle historical buildings and Alexandra knew how to handle a scalpel.

The plans all set, I sat down and looked at my watch. We still had two hours before we had to meet everyone. "Want to make a big breakfast?" I said. I needed to stay busy or this wait was going to get me all nervous again.

"I'll get the eggs and bacon. You start on the waffle mix?" Santi said as he headed for the fridge.

. . .

An hour and a half later, we were in the car on the way to my store. I wanted a little extra time to set up everything for everyone, and I still needed to do my opening chores for the store itself. It was going to be a busy day, and I was totally on board with that idea.

I cleared my desk of everything and set up a folding table next to it in my office. I didn't feel comfortable touching Saul's desk, even though he hardly used it, so I put another folding table in his office for people to use. Then, I pulled out our industrial-sized coffee pot and set a pot to brewing while I set out creamer, sugar, and spoons.

A few minutes later, Lucille and Dad rolled up, and Lucille came in carrying two trays of what looked to be the most decadent cinnamon rolls in the world. "Oh, my, those look good," Santi said.

"Got the recipe from a woman over at that bookstore you like in St. Marin's, Maryland, Pais. Thought today was the day to give them a try." Lucille set the trays down. "Now, where do I find paper plates?"

I pointed her to the back of the house where the kitchen had once been, and she returned with plates and extra napkins as well as a large knife. She immediately cut me a roll and told me to let her know how they were.

Given that I didn't slow down enough to talk until the roll was completely gone, I hoped I'd conveyed the message that they were delicious. I resisted the urge to have another, though, especially since I'd had two waffles, eggs, and bacon at home before we came. Research gave me an appetite.

Soon after, everyone else began to arrive, and as each person walked in I pointed out the coffee and cinnamon rolls and then told them my suggested research assignment. Everyone was totally on board with the plan, and once we'd all consumed Lucille's goodies and washed our hands, we got to work.

Tee and Lucille set up in my office with Ms. Nicholas, Alexandra, and me, while everyone else took their work to Saul's office. For the next few hours, we shouted our finds to each other across the central hallway, running back and forth to see any new information that seemed particularly relevant.

By the time we were set to start cooking the barbecue, the fence out front was decorated with the words *Women's Rights* in bright-yellow yarn, the posts on the front of the house were spun with a rainbow of color from top to bottom, and we had a pretty good theory about who our two Jemimas were and what exactly had been happening at the time Jemima Cavanaugh married Johnny Lanford.

But first, I wanted to thank everyone for their help and to give Mika's event a little push. So I asked everyone to gather by the front of the house, and then I stood on the porch and shouted, "Thank you," as loudly as I could. I had a momentary inclination to burst into song a la Elsa, but I suppressed the urge out of a desire to preserve a bit of my dignity.

"I'm so grateful to all of you for how you have rallied around our mystery today, and I'm excited to tell you that I think we have figured everything out." A small round of applause passed around the group. "Let me begin by telling you about Millie Cavanaugh."

For the next few minutes, I told the story of Millie and how she and her family had helped women escape abusive situations, how her daughter Jemima had taken up the charge, and how Jemima's husband Johnny had stepped in to help, too. Then, I told them about Millie's death, about how Jemima had felt the need to keep her relationship with Johnny a secret because she didn't want to put him in danger.

"We know all this thanks to the extensive research of Tee Black. Tee discovered, in an old journal kept at Lydia Baptist, that Jemima had told her whole story in those pages." This morning, when Tee had pulled out the journal and shown it to me, I had gasped. On the inside of the front cover was written, *Jemima Cavanaugh, spinster by choice*. I had laughed and felt a pang of sorrow at the same time when I read how she described her situation. She had chosen to protect her husband by not giving him a public tie to her.

He hadn't liked her decision, but he had respected it, which was why their marriage hadn't been formally registered with the county. *Johnny tried to tell me there was no threat that our love couldn't overcome*, Jemima had written, *but I knew that wasn't true. It hadn't been true for Mama and Daddy, and it wouldn't be true for us. Best to keep it a secret.*

As I spoke to my friends from the porch of the business I'd started on my own, with the man I loved beside me, I felt tears trickle down my cheeks. "Jemima was courageous like her mama, and when another young woman needed to feel brave, she took Jemima's name."

"What are you talking about?" a man's voice from the back of the group said.

I squinted against the sun shining in my face as I tried to see who was talking. The voice sounded familiar, but it wasn't familiar enough for me to identify right away. Santiago put a hand on my arm and then stepped off the porch and headed right, toward the man.

"I'm just sharing what we found this morning about Millie and Jemima Cavanaugh and Johnny Lanford," I said as I continued to peer into the sunshine. "I'm sorry, but who are you? I can't see you through the sun."

The man stepped forward, and as he moved closer, I saw it was Josh Lanford. "Oh, I'm so glad you're here, Josh," I said as I started to walk forward.

He moved closer to me, and only then did I see the scowl on his face. "You just said something about Grandma Jemima being a spinster. That's not true. She was married to my great-great-grandfather, Johnny. You told me that yourself."

I sighed. "You're right, I did. But I made a mistake. The woman whose marriage records you found took Jemima's name, but it wasn't the same woman named Jemima whose mother was Millie Cavanaugh."

Behind Josh, I could see Santiago edge closer while Saul and Dad gently moved Mika and Alexandra aside, too.

Meanwhile, Josh stepped up onto the porch and put himself between me and my friends gathered on the ground below. Suddenly, things felt a little dangerous, and I wasn't sure why. "I'm sorry I had jumped to the wrong conclusion when we talked yesterday," I said, hoping to diffuse the waves of anger coming off him.

"But you weren't wrong," he said. "You can't have been wrong because if you were wrong, then my great-great-grandfather wasn't Johnny Lanford." I could hear the crack in his voice now and realized that his anger was just a layer over a massive sadness.

I put my arm on his. "Oh, that is hard, isn't it?" I tried not to sound patronizing, but the last person I'd had to comfort with such hard feelings was my four-year-old son.

Josh didn't seem to mind, though, because he nodded as his face crumpled into tears. "Who am I then?" He stood there trembling as tears began to pour down his face.

Clearly something major was happening with Josh at this moment, more than simply learning that a man five generations ago wasn't his biological grandparent. Mika stepped onto the porch and slipped her arm around Josh's waist to lead him to the door.

Mary joined her and the two of them walked Josh inside as I turned back to my friends and more quietly said, "Josh is descended from a Jemima Lanford, but we gave him some bad information yesterday. I need to go clarify things for him."

Santi joined me on the porch after saying something to my dad and Saul, who promptly herded everyone to where the men had set up more folding tables near the cooker. Promptly, Tee, Lucille, and Ms. Nicholas began to open coolers and set out the food we had all brought to go with our barbecue. Everything well in hand there, Santi and I went inside.

Mika, Mary, and Josh sat at the table in my office, with Mary behind Josh, rubbing small circles on his back, and Mika sitting across from him, a glass of water in his hands. "So explain it to me again, one more time," he said.

Mika carefully walked him through the age difference between the women and about how Jemima Cavanaugh had a hysterectomy more than twenty years before Jemima Lanford gave birth. "It's just not physically possible that Jemima Cavanaugh was your grandmother." I could see Mika pacing the information, giving it to Josh in small chunks as his clearly overtaxed system could take it in.

I sat down beside him and laid my hand on his arm again. "It's really good you came by today because I was going to text you anyway. We know the name your great-great-grandmother had when she lived here in Octonia, and I think it may be good news for you."

Josh shook his head. "I'm sorry. This is a lot to take in." He sighed. "As long as I could remember, my dad has been so proud to be descended from Johnny Lanford, the gunslinging cowboy type. Some days, it was all we shared."

I took a deep breath. Josh's reaction made a lot more sense now. If he wasn't Johnny's great-grandson, he risked losing something with his dad. I understood that in my own way since I wished every day that I could ask my mom something about her side of the family, something that would tie me back to them in a richer way than paper records.

"Oh, that's so hard," I said to Josh. "What do you think your dad will make of this new information?" I asked quietly.

Josh started to cry again. "Nothing. He died six months ago."

I swallowed hard. "I'm so very sorry." This man had just lost his father, and today, we had told him that a precious connection with his dad was based on an inaccuracy. I wasn't sure what to say, but I knew that, in the end, the truth was always the best, so I said, "Your grandmother Jemima, she was a survivor, though."

Mary spoke as she continued to rub his back. "When you're ready to learn about her, we'll tell you all we can, okay?" She caught my eye, and I took her lead. He needed time.

"Thanks," he said. "It's weird, right? None of us knew Grandpa Johnny" – he winced at the familiar name as he corrected himself – "Johnny Lanford, but it's still painful, you know?"

"Not weird at all," I said. "I spend all day looking at people's old things and trying to recover the stories associated with those things because those stories matter. It doesn't matter that you didn't know Johnny. To you, he was Grandpa Johnny."

"And from what I know of him, I think he'd be just fine with you continuing to call him that," Mika added.

We sat quietly for a few minutes, and then Josh said, "I'm sorry to have barged in. I just came by to thank you for your help yesterday. But I can see I'm interrupting." He stood. "I'll see you another time."

"Will you stay for our barbecue? We have plenty to share." From the looks of what I could see from the windows as I stood, we had plenty for the entire county.

"Thank you," Josh said as he glanced outside, too. "But if it's not rude, I think I just need to be alone. Another time?"

I nodded. "Of course, and you have my number when you're ready to learn more – if you want to learn more."

Josh didn't resist when I gave him a quick hug, and when he had gotten into his car and left the lot, everyone turned to me for an update. I gave them as much of the story as I felt I could share, that Josh was a descendant of Jemima Lanford, but beyond that, the information was his to give, not mine.

After that hard moment, all I wanted to do was sit with my friends, drink a beer, and enjoy the afternoon. Fortunately, everyone else seemed to be of the same mind, and quickly, I got swept up into conversations about my shop, about yarn bombing, and most importantly, about Mika's event in one week. It was going to be a great event, and with everyone around totally dedicated to making it a huge success, I had no doubt we would not only help make Mika's financial goal but also raise some great money for Warm Up America.

As I was about to eat my second burger, Mika's boyfriend Chris joined us as a bit of a surprise. Normally weekends were his busiest time, but today he'd left business to his daughter so he could spend the evening with Mika. She beamed at him, and when they left a few minutes later, I just texted her a quick *Have a great night*. They got to see each other so rarely that I didn't want to intrude.

Mika's early departure meant that I could scheme a bit with our friends about how to boost her sales in the store even more. She was having a huge sale on almost all of her inventory, but a sale only worked if she sold a whole lot more stock than she normally would have. That meant we really had to get the traffic going into the shop and to her online store.

"I've already got the women from church coming to buy our yarn bombing supplies on Monday, and I'll remind them to buy a little extra for themselves," Mary said. "I'll also be making an announcement about the competition and the cause in church tomorrow."

Mary knew I already knew about these things, but I was glad she shared to get everybody going with ideas.

Saul, always the patron of the people he loved, said, "I'm going to buy a hundred skeins for yarn-workers who can't afford to buy their own, so please let people know they can be in touch with Mika to get free yarn if they need it."

I grinned. "That's a great idea," I said.

"I'll buy another twenty-five," Santi said.

"And we'll get fifty," Lucille said on behalf of herself and Dad.

"I still need to get our yarn for the historical society, so I'll stop by on my way home and pick some up," Ms. Nicholas said.

"We're doing the station, right?" Savannah asked.

"Do you think I could get away with *not* doing it?" Santi asked with a grin.

Savannah laughed. "Not a chance."

Alexandra cleared her throat and then said, "I don't know if this is too much, but if I could get a local TV station to announce the event and the store's mission for Warm Up America, would that be okay?"

"Okay?" Saul said. "That's more than okay. But let's keep it a surprise from Mika. Maybe you can hint, Pais, that she might want to stock up a bit extra so she has enough inventory?"

I nodded, but I'd have to be really sneaky so as to not tip Mika off. Maybe Santi could help me think of a plan tonight. "You have a special in with a local station?" I asked Alexandra.

She shrugged. "My brother is Anderson Chu," she said, naming one of the most popular anchors at the local Charlottesville television station.

"I didn't know that," I said. "How cool!"

"It is cool," she said, "just not something I share too often since I don't like being asked to ask him for favors. But in this case, I'm happy to ask, and I know he'll be happy to get a reporter up to talk to Mika for a story later in the week."

I grinned and gave her a quick high five. "I'm also going to make signs that explain about the blanket squares, Warm Up America, and Mika's shop so that people can hang them by their displays," I said.

"Bring them by the historical society offices when they're done, Paisley," Ms. Nicholas said. "We can laminate them to make them a bit more durable."

"I can't make any promises, but if I pull together a cake walk for the event, would anyone do that?" Lucille asked.

For a moment, I thought fondly of the one winning streak I'd had in my life. For four years in a row I had won the cake walk at my elementary school's fall festival. I raised my hand immediately and several other people followed suit.

"I love that idea, Lucille," Mary said. "We can organize that with the rest of the food. I'm sure some of the folks from church will contribute a cake."

With the food mostly eaten – an impressive feat, given the sheer amount of food that everyone had brought – and the beer almost gone, it seemed a logical time to pack up and head home. Everyone chipped in, and in a few minutes, the tables were stowed back in the run-in shed by the front of the lot, the trash put in the cans out back, and the house shut down and locked up.

I stopped Claire on her way to ask how the day's sales had been. I'd noticed a few customers going in and out throughout the day, but I'd been pretty distracted.

"Actually, great," Claire said. "Someone bought all those old windows we got from the abandoned house in town, and I sold a ton of odds and ends, including the taxidermized chipmunk. The woman who bought it was so excited. Said she would put it with her raccoon."

I shook my head. "It takes all kinds," I said as I gave Claire a hug. "Thank you for managing all that while we did our thing." I handed her a tote bag with a couple burgers, some of the potato salad, and a big slice of peanut butter pie. I'd been a twenty-something myself at one time, and I well-remembered the days when the gift of food was a reprieve from cereal for dinner.

She peeked in the bag. "Is that peanut butter pie?"

"Yes, ma'am," I said as I turned back toward the house. "Enjoy."

As all my friends followed her to their cars parked beside the house, Santiago stood on the porch, per our usual, and watched everyone go. Then, we loaded up and headed home for a quiet night of wedding planning.

The flowers finally picked – sunflowers with lots of zinnias and dahlias – and the decision to hire a DJ finalized so that we could save ourselves all the work of picking music, Santiago and I settled in to watch *Schitt's Creek* for the first time. We had heard the rave reviews, and we figured, after discussing the issue, that we were aware enough of our own small communities foibles to appreciate someone else both making fun of them and honoring them, too. We weren't wrong. Two episodes in, we were hooked.

As we watched, I made a lot of progress on my latest cross-stitch project, another Teresa Wentzler, this time a paisley pattern that Lucille had bought me as a sort of joke. But the pattern itself was beautiful, and I looked forward to hanging it when I was done in approximately twenty-eight years.

8

The next morning, after staying up way too late watching the Levy men crack us up, I got dressed in a long skirt, peasant blouse, and boots for church. It was the most fancy I ever got, and even for church, I usually opted for pants and a nicer knit shirt. But today, Mary was making her announcement about Mika's event, and I wanted to look good for both of my friends.

Santiago headed out about the same time I did to pick up his mom for Mass down in Charlottesville, and we made plans to meet back up at his place that afternoon. Santiago had some weeding to do, he said, and he hoped I would keep him company while I sewed. It sounded like a delightful way to relax on a Sunday afternoon.

But first, we had to pump up the church crowd for Mika's event. Our church didn't necessarily need much help in getting pumped up. Our organist always brought us in with a rousing old-school hymn, and the singing was rich with hand-clapping that I could, in no way, master. But this was the first time in the over a year that I had been attending that anyone talked about a service project.

It wasn't that the folks at Bethel didn't do service projects. They did – a lot of them, including running a Meals on Wheels program out of the church fellowship hall, offering tutoring programs to kids in the afternoons, and maintaining the local community garden. But those things had been established as part of the church community for a long time. Mika's event was totally new, and I was a little nervous that church members might resent a white lady asking for help. After all, white people had relied on the "help" of black people for a long time, a fact that all the members of Bethel, besides Mika and I, knew far too well from experience.

What I forgot in my fretting, of course, was that the people of Bethel were generous beyond belief. When Mary made her announcement at the end of the service, Mika was nearly swallowed up in the crowd of folks gathering to ask when they could come to buy yarn, what they could provide for the bake sale, and could she make a note of their yarn bombing projects right now so they could get started right away?

Fortunately, Mary had thought ahead and brought a pad and pen, and she was steadily writing down what everyone offered so that she could distribute information as needed later on. For my part, I stood next to Mika, smiling and helping to hold her up against the surge of helpfulness that continued for well over a half hour.

By the time the three of us started to walk to Mary's house for our usual lunch, Mika had at least a dozen new yarn bomb entries, a page-long list of baked goods, and promises of dozens of purchases from her store tomorrow. She was practically floating down the sidewalk.

Unlike most weeks, Mary had decided to keep our lunch to just the three of us so that we could talk a bit more about the research findings from the day before. "We just need to sit with this stuff, you know?" she had said the night before when she called. "I'll make pot roast next week to make it up to folks."

That was a big "make-up," if you asked me. Mary made the *best* pot roast I had ever tasted, and I considered myself a pot roast connoisseur.

Now, with our big plates full of salad and chicken-and-mushroom casserole, another of Mary's best dishes, we sat down at her table. As we all ate our first few bites, silence surrounded us and I felt the importance of all we'd found yesterday finally settle into my body. We had discovered a pretty incredible story of bravery, one that built on Millie and Jemima Cavanaugh's legacy, and I was eager to talk about it.

But I couldn't figure out how to begin because I kept getting stuck on the fact that this story meant not only did Josh Lanford lose the connection to a truly inspiring man but also that he gained an abusive reprobate of a great-great-grandfather instead.

"How do we tell Josh about his actual grandfather?" I said, deciding to begin where I was, with the hard stuff.

Mary shook her head. "I don't know, girls. But we have to tell him. He's going to find out soon, when your article goes out, Paisley. He deserves to be told in person."

I nodded, and Mika said, "Maybe we should invite him to the shop this week, tell him about his family's history, and see how we plan to honor both his great-grandmother and Jemima Cavanaugh."

I smiled. "That's a great idea. Maybe we can do a little private reception in their honor, ask Josh to bring any of his family that he wants."

With this plan clarified, I was able to move past the contemporary problem and go back into history to Jemima Lanford, Josh's great-great-grandmother, the woman who had fled from the most powerful man in Octonia and lived to tell the tale.

At least that's how Tee had put it when she'd shared the letter from "Jemima Two," as we were now calling her, in the church's records. She and Ms. Nicholas had put together a whole history of Jemima Two, née Meredith Gilbert, and presented it to the rest of us in my office the day before. The story was heartbreaking and inspiring, and I hoped with all my heart that Josh could see it the way we did, even as he realized this meant he shared DNA with a rather despicable figure.

Apparently, Jemima Two had been married off, by her impoverished parents, when she was just sixteen. The situation, from what we could tell, seemed impossible since they had three younger girls to care for and very little means, since Jemima Two's father had lost a hand in a farming accident, to provide for themselves.

So when they promised their young daughter to Franklin Margen, the wealthiest man in the county, the man who owned the local country store and the grain mill, they had received a hefty dowry in return. According to Jemima Two's letter, she had encouraged her parents to take what Margen offered because she knew it would give them the means to care for her younger sisters and, perhaps, find them more loving partners in the world. "I told them to 'do what is best for the most,'" she told Jemima One, years later.

With that missive, she had left home and moved in with a man who beat her, starved her, and confined her to home most days. Apparently, this went on for almost two years, until Jemima Two found out she was pregnant. Then, she knew she had to get out, and so she sent a letter – apparently via Johnny Lanford – to Jemima Cavanaugh and asked for her help.

It was that letter that Tee and Ms. Nicholas found, and it was that letter that helped them track down the rest of Meredith Gilbert's story. By the time they told the rest of us about her, they knew her birthdate, that she'd been raised out in the hollows near Octonia Mill, and that she was one of four girls, all of the rest of whom had gone on to make, as best they could tell, good marriages.

They couldn't find any information on Jemima Two's escape

from Margen, but she showed up as *Jemima Lanford* on the Charlottesville city directories the following year. At the next census, she was working as a housekeeper and marked as head of household with her young son. From there, the family line was clear as day all the way down to Josh.

As I helped myself to a second helping of casserole, I said, "Do you think we can find any pictures of Jemima Two? Or of Johnny, her son?"

Mika tilted her head and looked at me. "You're asking us, Ms. History?"

I smiled. "Right. Okay, let's see if we can. Maybe he showed up in the newspaper or something?"

Mary nodded. "I'll put some time to it this afternoon, but now, Ms. Sutton, I do believe you have a date with a very fine man."

I smiled. "I do, indeed," I said as I stood up and carried my plate into the kitchen. "Can I help you clean up before I go?"

"I'll stay and then walk home," Mika said. "It's a nice day for a walk, and it'll give me a chance to relax a little before I begin compiling these orders for the folks tomorrow."

I smiled, hugged both my friends, and then walked back to my car up the street toward the church.

9

When I pulled up in front of Santi's house, he was waiting for me on the front lawn. His knees were dirty like he'd been weeding away for quite a while, and the grin on his face told me he was in his happy place.

But when I climbed out of the car and he took a wide step to the right, revealing a big *Sold* placard on top of a real estate sign that hadn't been there a week ago, I understood this joy was about more than just pulling weeds. "You sold your house?" I said.

"I did. We'd talked about it, and I wanted to surprise you." He leaned over and kissed me after my slightly dazed walk to him. "Sawyer helped me finalize everything during our dinner date the other night. I wanted to be sure he understood what was happening."

Tears pooled in my eyes. This man was so thoughtful, and even though he had never been a parent before, he was parenting my son so well. "What did Saw say?"

Santiago grinned. "He said he would play with me all the time."

I laughed. "Well, it's good he's trying to make you comfortable with the situation," I said.

"I think so," Santi said before he stepped closer and caught my gaze. "Are you comfortable with the situation?"

I looked at him and then over at his lovely house. It was so beautiful, and part of me would be sad to see it go. But the three of us belonged at my house; I felt that deep inside myself. I grinned. "I think I can tolerate it," I said, and kissed him deeply. "Now, tell me about the plan."

As we walked around his beautiful landscape, he told me that the sellers wanted to close in two weeks and hoped it would be okay for him to move in that quickly. I, of course, said that was fine and that we were going to use his couch since Beauregard had recently shredded another cushion from mine.

But then, Santi said, "And I'd like to take the proceeds of the sale and do a few things, if it's okay with you."

I stopped walking and looked at him. His tone had gotten very serious, and I knew I needed to see his face while he shared his plans. "Okay," I said. "What are you thinking?"

"First, I own this house outright, so the selling price, minus closing costs, is what I'll make from the sale." He told me the figure, and I was glad we'd stopped by a chair in his yard because I needed to sit down. "So first, I'd like to pay off your house and get us out from under that mortgage."

I stared at him and somehow managed to say, "Let me hear your whole plan before I agree to anything." Not that I didn't want to agree, but it was best that I get the whole deal before committing to any part of it, lest I have a heart attack caused by unconditional love. Then, we'd need to work from my will, and that seemed complicated at this point.

He smiled. "Then, I'd like to set up an emergency fund for all of us so that we're all set if something major happens."

"Uh-huh," I sputtered.

"Then, I'd like to split the rest between Sawyer's education now and his education in the future." He explained that he knew I'd wanted to send Sawyer to a school that had a more experiential aspect than most public schools were able to provide, and that now, he hoped we could do that as well as setting up Saw's college fund so he could afford whatever school he wanted when the time came.

It was the *we* in his sentences that finally broke me down, and I started to cry. I never thought that someone helping me care for the financial future would be the deepest testament to love I'd ever experienced, but here it was. This man was giving up his home, and he hadn't set aside a single bit of the money from its sale to do something for himself.

When I told him that, he said, "Paisley, marrying you and Sawyer, that's all for me, woman. All for me."

At that point, I couldn't even cry anymore, so I just got up and did a little leaping run around his backyard, trying to let my joy show as much as possible for his sake and for the eyes of the slightly nosy woman who lived next door. She was actually wonderful, but I loved giving her something to talk about. I figured a leaping middle-aged woman would hold her for a few days.

When I finally settled, all the excitement and overwhelmed leapt out of me, I said, "I agree, but on one condition."

"What's that?" he said.

"We take some of the money and buy you a motorcycle with a sidecar for Saw." I knew this had been a dream of Santi's for a long time, and I also knew that unless I required it of him, he would never do it.

His face split wide open. "Deal."

For the next few minutes, we gave the nosy neighbor a bit more to talk about as we celebrated this news – and each other – a bit passionately. But then, he said, "I do really want to weed so that the place looks great for the new owners. Did you bring your cross-stitch?"

I stared at him again. "Are you actually thinking I'm going to sit here and calmly sew while you work on a house that will make my wildest dreams come true?"

"Um, yeah," he said.

"You are out of your mind, sir," I said as I headed toward my car. "Just let me put on my jeans." I had actually been planning to help him weed all along, knowing I would feel too guilty just sitting while he worked, but now I was super glad I had packed a change of clothes.

For the next two hours, we pulled out ground ivy and rogue dandelions, and by the time we were done, the beds that surrounded Santi's luxurious backyard were perfect. The new owners wouldn't have much maintenance to do until next spring, and I knew that was a true gift.

On the way home, I texted Saw's dad and offered to pick him up, if that would suit, and soon, we had the boy in the back of the car and talking nonstop about the deer he had snuck up on and how he'd gone swimming in the "huge" lake. Finally, Sawyer took a breath, and Santi said, "I told your mom our secret, Saw. She's in."

I turned to look at my son in the back seat. "You did a really good job of keeping the secret," I said.

"Santi said I could have two eggs if I did." Saw said, "And I knew it would make you happy, Mama."

Again, tears filled my eyes, but I quickly wiped them away. "Two eggs?" I said with a laugh to Santi. "This kid may deserve three."

Sawyer pumped the air with his fist. "I'm going to eat them all up."

"Not at once," I said. "Pace yourself."

Sawyer rolled his eyes, and I felt time flash forward ten years. Oh, he was going to be quite the teenager, but now, Santi would be there beside me for all that eye rolling. That made everything seem exciting.

. . .

THE NEXT MORNING after dropping Sawyer off at school, I headed into my office to write my article about Millie, Jemima, and all the women they had helped, including Avery Humboldt and Meredith Gilbert. I wasn't planning on sending it out until Thursday, after the reception with the Lanfords on Wednesday night, but I knew we had a busy week ahead with preparing for Mika's event. I didn't want to leave this to the last minute.

I wrote the article quite quickly, but as I crafted the announcement about Mika's Women of the Skein event, I realized that I needed to get word out about that much sooner than Thursday if I wanted people to act. So I scheduled this newsletter with the story for after the reception, but I went ahead and wrote up a quick note to encourage my readers to plan ahead for Saturday and the yarn bombing festivities. I added a teaser about the theme, too, and said, *Also, come here about some of the most amazing women in Octonia's history and how they can inspire us all.*

I hit send and hoped that my readers, who were almost all enthusiastic supporters of the local community, would turn out in force for Mika. Then, I forwarded the email link to Mika and Mary and asked them to post it to their social media.

I heard back from Mary immediately, who was quite willing to share the link far and wide, but then she said, *Can you come downtown in a bit? I think Mika could use your help.*

Claire was due at the shop in fifteen minutes, so I said I'd be right over and asked what was up.

You'll see, Mary's text said, and I took that to be good news, something that involved a good sales day and not a total dearth of customers that had sent my best friend into sadness.

Claire was right on time, as usual, and after letting her know everything was ready for business, I jumped in my car and rushed downtown. Since I had to park down the street instead of in front of Mika's shop like I typically did, I figured that maybe the news was encouraging. Either that, or there was some highly-publicized trial at the courthouse that I had, not surprisingly, missed since I never watched or read the news, at least from my own lifetime.

Fortunately, the downtown crowd *was* there for Mika, and when I walked in the shop, I could see immediately why Mary had suggested I come. The store was packed. Mrs. Stephenson and Mika were both helping customers, and the line at the register was already five deep. As I made my way to the counter to ring up sales, I greeted the women from church and the other friends from the area that I knew, and then I got to work.

The purchases ranged from dozens of skeins of yarn for a particularly large project to just a couple of small skeins of lace-yarn for doilies. One woman bought five skeins of a really beautiful silk yarn and said she was getting it because it was expensive and so she'd feel obligated to finally learn how to make a scarf.

An hour after I arrived, the number of customers in the store finally thinned, and Mika came over to thank me. "How did you know to come?" she asked. "I was going to text you, but I couldn't even get a minute to do that."

"Mary told me. I figured you must have talked to her," I said as my friend looked at me with a very confused expression.

"Nope, I didn't have a chance to talk to anyone." She turned as the bell over the door rang again, and Mary walked in. "We were just talking about you," Mika said.

"I got here as quickly as I could. I can't stay long, but given the number of messages I was getting with pictures of the beautiful yarn people were buying, I figured you were swamped."

I laughed. "That's how you knew. I thought maybe you were psychic."

Mary smiled. "Only if being on everyone's contact list

makes me so." She looked around. "Looks like you could use some help restocking."

Mika sighed. "Yeah. I'm glad I got a big order this morning, but I haven't even opened it yet." She raised her voice to Mrs. Stephenson. "You okay for a few minutes?"

"I've got it, Mika," she said. "Take a break."

Mika laughed out loud. "I'm just going to unpack our order. Be back in a minute."

The three of us made our way to the back room, and when I saw the eight huge boxes that we needed to unpack, I was extra glad we had six hands instead of just Mika's two. Quickly, we found the packing slips and began organizing the yarn by type.

Then, we carried out armfuls of yarn and began filling the bins. By the time Mary's lunch break was over, most of the stock was on the floor, and the stream of customers was back. "Wish I could stay longer," Mary said.

"I think we've got it," I told her. "Thanks for giving me a heads-up."

Mika hugged her quickly. "Yes, thanks. Oh, and tomorrow night, let's meet here to talk about the reception."

Mary smiled and hustled out the door around a group of five women, all wearing what appeared to be handmade clothing. It was going to be a banner sales day for my friend, that was for sure.

About midafternoon, after she required Mrs. Stephenson to take lunch, I forced Mika to take her own break. While she was gone, Mrs. Stephenson ran the register while I re-tidied the floor and answered as many questions as I could. When Mika came back, everything was in tip-top shape again, and I felt confident she could handle things for the rest of the day.

That was good because we still hadn't contacted Josh about the reception in two days. Mika and I had thought maybe I should call him, but before I did, I'd wanted to check with her about the details. Between customers, I jotted down everything about the event, and then I snuck into the back room and gave him a call.

"Hi Josh. This is Paisley Sutton," I said when he picked up. "Do you have a minute?"

"Sure. I'm actually glad you called. I was hoping I might find you at your shop, but your assistant said you'd headed downtown. Do you have time for a cup of coffee?" he asked.

I glanced out the backroom door and saw that Mika and Mrs. Stephenson had things well in hand, but I still hesitated. The last time I'd talked to Josh, it had been pretty intense. Still, I was curious about what he had to say, and he didn't sound upset at the moment. "Sure," I said. "Coffee shop in ten minutes?"

"Sounds good. I'm on my way there now."

I hung up the phone and decided to go on over. For some reason, I thought it might be better that he not know I had been at Mika's shop for the day.

As I walked across the street, I tried to think through why I didn't want him to know that, especially since he was, hopefully, going to be in that very shop in about forty-eight hours, but I couldn't give myself a rational reason. Fortunately, rationality wasn't the only reasoning I listened to these days, so I let myself off the hook.

I ordered my decaf latte and sat down at the table by the window. Then, following that same intuition that had kept me from telling Josh about my time at Mika's store, I texted Santiago to let him know where I was and suggest that if he had a minute he might wander by.

His reply was immediate. *I'll drop in casually in ten minutes. See you then.*

Then, I eschewed all the social media and played my candy matching game to let my nervous system settle just a bit. I was definitely anxious about something, but since I didn't have enough information yet to know what, I decided that I'd do my best to not appear anxious to the person who was, for unknown reasons, making me feel that way.

When Josh walked in just a few moments later, I was calmer but on guard. He smiled at me as he went to the counter, and when he turned with two cups in his hands, I found myself glad they had lids on them. It was an instinctual reaction, but it gave me a clue to what my intuition was saying. Clearly, I thought Josh might hurt me.

As he sat down and slid my drink across the table, I glanced back toward the counter and saw that the barista was putting lids on all the drinks, and I let myself relax just a little. I wasn't going to be ruffled today, it seemed. Still, I didn't let my guard all the way down. Something was up with Josh.

"I want to apologize for the way I acted yesterday," he said after taking a sip of his coffee. "I was just caught off guard." He smiled, but the gesture didn't reach his eyes.

My alerts went back up a notch. "I totally understand," I said as sincerely as I could. "It's a lot to take in when you find out your family history is vastly different from what you thought it was."

He nodded. "Here's the thing, though. You're wrong." He looked me in the eyes as he said that last sentence, and he wasn't smiling anymore.

I forced myself to swallow my sip of latte, and then I said, "I'm sorry?"

"You're wrong. Johnny Lanford is my great-great-grandfather. I know that probably bruises your ego as the all-knowing historian of Octonia, but there it is." He raised his eyebrows and looked at me over his cup as he took another sip.

Years on social media had taught me there was no value in arguing with someone who was so sure of their own rightness, so I simply let out a long sigh and sat back. This is why I had been on guard. My body had known this conversation wasn't going to be casual.

As I sat there and tried to think of a response, Santiago walked in, ordered a coffee, and then turned around as if he was just waiting for his drink when he spotted me. "Hey, Woman. What are you doing here?" my fiancé asked as he walked over. Then he looked at Josh. "Oh, hi, Josh, good to see you again. You guys talking about history?"

I looked at Santiago and let my eyes go very wide, hoping Santi would see my shock in my expression. "Exactly," I said. "Josh was just telling me that he has concluded we are wrong about the identity of his great-great-grandfather."

Santi pulled his head back a little. "Oh yeah?" He grabbed a chair from a nearby table and then sat down with his legs braced around its back. "Tell me more."

Josh visibly relaxed, and I felt a bit of my tension slide off me, too. The age-old "tell me more" was almost always a good response to something someone said, and it worked here because Josh leaned forward and started talking.

"Well, first, there's just no way Jemima would name her child Johnny if she wasn't naming him after the boy's father." Josh tapped one finger on the table and then added a second. "Then, you take in the fact that her name was Jemima, just like Johnny's wife." He looked up at me. "You're the one who showed me the marriage certificate."

I started to explain, but I felt Santiago's foot nudge mine under the table and nodded instead.

"Finally, there's the fact that I look just like him, same hair, same eyes, same everything. He has to be my relative." Josh sat back as if he had just made a clean-cut case in a court of law, despite the fact that all of his arguments were based on the presumption that Johnny Lanford needed to be proven to be his grandfather rather than coming to knowledge from the facts that existed.

I glanced over at Santi, and I could see a bit of color at the tips of his ears. This kind of faulty logic was one of his pet peeves. It's why he always insisted on following the evidence instead of his own presumptions.

Santi looked at me and gave me a small nod. "I'm afraid, Josh, that you're simply wrong about this, but I don't say that with any malice. In fact, if you'd like to join me at the yarn shop across the street Wednesday night, we can walk you through the evidence we have. Maybe you'd like to invite your family along, too." Given the circumstances, this event was not going to be the casual reception we'd hoped for, but we couldn't control the circumstances.

And while I didn't really feel any obligation to prove what we knew to be fact to this man, he was a member of our community, and I still wanted to give him a chance to come to terms with this information before it went public. It was his family, after all, and while facts didn't change because the story was in his DNA, I did want to give him a little extra space to understand.

Josh studied me for a minute, and then he said, "You're on. Dueling history, if you will. You present your 'facts.'" He made air quotes around the word *facts*. "I'll present mine." He stood up. "What time?"

"Six. We'll provide food. Invite whoever you like, and we'll do the same." I could hear the sharpness in my voice, but I didn't care. I was trying to be kind, but this kind of willful ignorance – where we want something to be true just because we want it – pushed my buttons.

"See you then," he said as he turned and walked out the door.

"Ba da bink, bink, bink, bink, bink, bink, bink," Santi sang as he pretended to play the banjo like the kid in *Deliverance.*

I squinted at him. "What's that about?"

"Dueling history ... Dueling banjos," he said. "Get it?"

I rolled my eyes. "I get it. I get it."

"Maybe you should organize a canoe trip for beforehand

just to get into the right spirit," Santi said as he helped me to my feet.

"Hardy, har, har," I said, but I was smiling. It was going to be an intense couple of days even before we needed to prove every piece of information we had. We could do it, but gracious, I had been looking forward to a glass of wine and some stuffed mushroom caps. Now, I was going to have to do PowerPoint and stick to water until my presentation was done. Bummer!

Dad and Lucille met us at home an hour later with Sawyer. They'd offered to pick him up when I'd explained how swamped Mika's store had been, and it had turned out to be a good thing since I'd had to contend with the man who refused to believe the truth, which was how I was now thinking of Josh Lanford.

As usual, Sawyer had a lot to say, so Santi and I spent the first twenty minutes letting him spin out his tales from the school day before all the boys went out to play T-ball, at my request, so that Lucille and I could make dinner.

She'd brought over a big loaf of crusty bread, and I'd pulled out the tomato sauce and mozzarella. It was time for rustic pizza, and so while we sliced mushrooms and laid them on some thick slices of her good bread, I told her about my conversation with Josh.

While she had her back turned to me as she slid the tray of bread into the oven, she said, "And you're absolutely sure you have your facts right, Paisley?"

My brain knew she was asking out of kindness, wanting to be sure I wasn't going to be publicly humiliated on Wednesday evening, but the tired, stressed part of me was defensive. So I snapped, "Of course I have all my facts right. What are you saying, Lucille?" I stretched out her name with my anger, and I almost suggested she finish dinner while I went upstairs to mope.

But then she turned around with a grin on her face. "That's my girl," she said. "All fight. You go get 'em."

With her enthusiastic vigor behind me, I felt the strain and self-doubt I had been having about her very question subside. I did know I was right. I knew that Tee and Ms. Nicholas were right, and I knew that Josh Lanford was holding onto a fantasy because it was painful to let it go. Right then and there, I decided that while I wasn't going to hold back on what I had to say, I also wasn't going to be cruel. He could think of the evening's event as a contest if he wanted. I was going to consider it a conversation.

But tonight, I was going to have wine, so I poured Lucille and myself a glass and led her to the porch, where we sat down to watch the four-year-old school the older guys in how to hit a ball off a stick. Sawyer was, as usual, profoundly adept with his body, and while Dad and Santi weren't physical slouches, they were both panting by the time Sawyer had sent them all over the field to get the balls he hit.

Eventually, they all quit and joined us on the porch. Sawyer took his bulldozer and began to pile up the scatterings of leaves that were beginning to litter the porch, and Santi went inside to grab himself and Dad a beer. It was going to be cool tonight, but for now, the porch was a perfect temperature.

As we all talked about Mika's event, Lucille filled us in on what she was going to provide by way of baked goods – baklava, her famous rugelach, and chocolate chip cookies. "I think those will complement the beef stroganoff and salad that Mary is bringing."

My mouth was already watering at the thought, and we still had another ten minutes on for the pizza. "That sounds amazing," I said. "Simple and delicious," I added. "Feels perfect for a craft-related event."

"Sounds perfect for any event," Dad said. "How many people will be at this thing?" My dad was the quintessential introvert, especially since large crowds were hard for him because of his limited hearing. He always wanted to prepare psychologically for bigger groups.

"I really have no idea, Dad. But it could be pretty big. Just depends on how many people enter the competition or come to see if they win a door prize," I said. As I said that, I realized that our plan to hold the prize announcement and dinner at Mika's shop probably wasn't going to work. She just didn't have the room. "Think Saul will let us have it at the lot?"

"Are you kidding?" Dad said. "That guy would do anything for you, kind of like your old man."

I knew Dad was right, but I also knew I needed to ask. So I quickly texted Mika to see if she was okay with the change in location, and when she expressed relief at not having to figure out how to host what was now forty-two entrants and their friends in her shop, I called Saul. The man could text, but he really preferred a phone call.

By the time the timer went off on the pizza, we had a new location and the promise of bulldozer rides for the kids at Saul's suggestion. The event was getting better and better.

Now, I just had to make it through Wednesday and Josh Lanford's hostility to get there. I'd worry about that later. Now, I had some pizza to eat and a toddler to coerce into trying a mushroom.

10

Tuesday was my day to run the shop since Claire had that day off, and with Saw at school all day, I could catch up on some of the work I'd been neglecting for the past week. I had payroll to do for myself and Claire, and I needed to update my online inventory and refresh my auction listings. Plus, my bookkeeping could use a little tending.

Since those kinds of tasks were not my strong suit, they required all my attention. I could get very absorbed in what I was doing, so I asked Santiago to come get me at noon so I wouldn't work right through lunch.

I was well into balancing my books when I saw the denim-clad legs of someone standing in front of my desk. I looked up with a start and saw a woman with a long, dark braid, brown freckles across her pale nose, and a broad-brimmed hat on her head. The combination of the way she was standing with her legs wide apart and the hat made me immediately think of the Wild West. If she'd been wearing a silver pistol on her hip, I would not have been surprised.

I stood up and said, "I'm sorry. I didn't hear you come in. Paisley Sutton." I put out my hand. "How can I help you?"

The woman gave my hand a single hard shake and said, "I'm Mickey Lanford. I think my brother Josh has been talking with you." Her voice was rich and full, and I wondered if she was a singer.

"Nice to meet you," I said as I came around my desk. "Yes, Josh and I have had a couple of conversations." I studied her face a minute but then decided to just be forthright. "We don't exactly understand your family's history the same way."

She shook her head. "You say that kindly, but my brother can be a real idiot. I told him years ago that his and Daddy's obsession with us being kin to Johnny Lanford was ridiculous. Sure, he sounds like he was a good guy, but what did that have to do with us? We're good people on our own right."

I smiled. "I understand that, completely. But some people really put a lot of stake in their family stories. I guess your brother and father are two of those people."

"I suppose so," she said as she looked around the room. "But you'd like that when someone who knows as much as you do tells them they're wrong, they'd believe you. Sorry Josh has made this into such a to-do. He's been listening to Daddy too long."

"He mentioned that he and your dad were close, so I get it. Losing a parent and then something you and that parent shared can be tough." I thought about how my mom had taught me to cross-stitch and about how long it took me to pick the hobby back up after she died.

Mickey looked at me strangely. "Are you thinking that our daddy is dead?"

I nodded as I thought back to my conversation with Josh on Saturday. "I'm sorry. I must have misunderstood your brother."

She pointed at the chair beside the window. "Mind if we sit?" she asked.

I shook my head and sat down in the chair on the other side of the window. "So your father is still alive."

"Oh, very much so. Just saw him earlier today at bingo, in fact. I take him every Tuesday. He was making a ruckus about showing you the 'errors of your ways' tomorrow night. That's why I stopped by. Wanted to give you a heads-up that he and Josh are coming, guns a-blazing." She shook her head. "I'm not sure I know the ins and outs, but from what I hear, you're only talking about the facts."

"I am. But like I said, I get it. It can be hard to find a family story isn't quite what you thought it was." I looked out the window and then back at her. "I take it you aren't as attached to Johnny Lanford as your dad and brother."

She shrugged. "Honestly, don't care much either way. History isn't really my thing." She looked at me quickly. "No offense."

"None taken," I said. "Lots of things aren't my thing, like makeup, for example." I stared at the bare-faced woman in front of me.

She laughed and put out a fist for me to bump. "I like you," she said. "Glad I came by."

"Thanks for the heads-up." I leaned forward a little. "I want you to know that I'm not trying to prove your brother wrong or anything. I started this conversation to give him a warning so that he wouldn't be surprised when the story gets more public."

"I appreciate that," she said. "I'll be there tomorrow, do my best to keep Daddy and Josh in line. But they can be pretty rowdy when it comes to what they think they know." She sighed and cracked her knuckles.

"Seems like you have experience with what they think they know," I said, hoping I wasn't prying too much with this woman I had just met.

She rolled her eyes. "Dinners in our house were always intense. Daddy liked to play devil's advocate and challenged every single thing we said we had learned. Josh took after Daddy, and I took off the other way." She sighed again. "Neither of them trust experts, especially if those experts are women. I've been a vet for fifteen years, and they still don't believe I can take care of their dogs. Haul those poor creatures half an hour away to see some old guy who hasn't learned anything new about caring for animals since 1972."

"I know some folks like that," I said, thinking of how stubborn my dad and Saul could be about what they knew. "Most of the time there's no harm in that, and really, there's no harm in your dad and brother thinking Johnny Lanford is their ancestor. I just know different is all. And since I'm writing a newsletter about it—"

She interrupted me. "You don't have to explain. I've been trying to tell my daddy to stop feeding his dogs onions for years now, and one day, his dogs are going to die. Then, he'll ask me why I didn't tell him not to do that." She shook her head. "Sometimes, there is just no room for truth, you know."

I did know. Far too well.

As both of us sat staring out the window, I had a sudden urge to tell her about the bones under the Cavanaugh family chicken coop. Somehow, I thought she might be able to shed some light on who that person was, but given that we'd just discussed the fact that her family wasn't really kin to either the Cavanaughs or the Lanfords, I chalked my urge up to stress and wanting to find some answers about that. I let the urge pass.

A moment later, she stood. "I'll see you tomorrow night, Paisley. I'll have your back, too." She shook my hand again and sauntered out the door. I almost felt like she was walking into the sunset instead of into the hallway outside my office just before I heard a big ole diesel truck pull away.

WHEN SANTI SHOWED up a bit later for lunch, I was still trying to regain focus on my financials. But I found myself really struggling since I couldn't help but think about the reception-turned-contest the next night. I appreciated Mickey's warning, but it had also made me more anxious. What kind of situation was I creating with this event tomorrow? It was too late to cancel now, but I kind of wished I could.

I told Santi about Mickey's visit and my nervousness, and he assured me that he would be there with Savannah or Brett to be sure police presence was clear. "We might be enough to keep the Lanford men under wraps, but I imagine Mickey can do that herself. Daughters have a way of taming their fathers and brothers."

I smiled because I knew how Santi felt about his sister. She was a force, one that didn't need her big brother to take care of her at all, and yet Santi still felt responsible for his Nina, as he called her.

With the promise of Santi's presence, his assurances about Mickey, and my own confidence in our research, I decided to table my concerns and instead concentrate on inviting a few people who had a place in the conversation, namely Jonathan Boykins, Jackie, Mary, Tee Black, Alexandra, and Ms. Nicholas. If we were going to open this up to a more public forum, then it was only right that everyone involved in both the history and the research was invited.

When we got back from lunch, I sat down and typed out a text invitation to the people I thought should be there, and within the next hour, they all said they'd come. Jonathan was particularly excited because he wanted to learn more about Millie and Jemima, his ancestors. I wasn't sure he'd be thrilled to hear the Lanfords' rendition of history, but I trusted in the gracious spirit he'd extended to me. It was all going to be fine.

11

By the time five p.m. Wednesday rolled around, I was a jumble of nerves, an over-rehearsed mess, and a jittery bundle of energy who had consumed far too much caffeine. I'd spent the day revising (and revising again) my PowerPoint slides, and now that it was time to actually set up the portable projector I used on the rare occasions when I was invited to give talks, I couldn't even get the cords into the jacks.

Santi took over for me and told me to go sit in the Cozy Nook, have something decaf to drink, and take a few deep breaths. I nodded and did as I was told. Mika was busy helping Lucille and Saul set up the refreshments, and Dad was keeping Sawyer busy with chalk on the sidewalk out front. When things got started, they would take Sawyer to my house since he wasn't great at sitting through a presentation, and I was grateful they'd made the suggestion.

Savannah showed up early and in uniform, and I was grateful to see her take a seat between the door and the stage so that everyone who came in saw her. I knew that wasn't an incidental choice on her part.

Right at six, the crowd began to enter the shop. First

Jonathan Boykins and a woman about his age in a black leather corset matching his leather kilt arrived. He gave me a wave and took a seat in the middle of the room. Then Mary and Tee Black came in with Ms. Nicholas soon after. Alexandra came in next and sat right next to Savannah. Finally, Josh and Mickey Lanford arrived, each holding an arm of an older man in a tie, Army cap with Vietnam War insignia, and gray dress pants. Clearly, this was Jonas Lanford.

I walked over to the Lanfords and introduced myself to their father. Mickey smiled and said, "It's nice to see you, Paisley. Thanks for organizing this."

Josh shot his sister a glare, and their dad put out his hand to me. "Ms. Sutton, I appreciate this chance to defend our family's honor. No hard feelings, I hope."

I stifled a smile and said, "Of course not. May the truth prevail." I turned away to go and take my seat, but I had to work hard not to let my nerves overcome. I felt a bit like I was a knight going into a joust, only against an old man whose feelings I really didn't want to hurt.

Mika welcomed us all to her shop, reminded everyone that there were refreshments, and gave everyone a few details about the Women of the Skein event on Saturday. "We'll be honoring three of the women we're going to talk about here tonight: Millie Cavanaugh, Jemima Cavanaugh, and Jemima Lanford. I hope you can all join us."

As she spoke, a few more people straggled in, and when Josh waved to a couple of young men and an old woman who all had the same dark hair as he and his sister did, I guessed that more of the Lanford contingent had arrived. Only then did I think I should have suggested Jonathan invite his family, too, but it was too late for that. Maybe they'd come on Saturday.

Mika turned to Josh and introduced him, using the prepared notes he'd sent me earlier in the day. He described himself as a family historian and stickler for the truth, a turn of phrase which made me want to cringe and laugh all at the same moment.

I had offered to let Josh go first by saying that I wanted to be courteous to his family and give them the first word, but I also knew that people tended to remember the last thing they heard in a presentation. So I was hoping the facts about the Cavanaugh and Lanford families would stick with people more than the history Josh was presenting.

To his credit, he gave an enthusiastic presentation, including photos of the old UVA hospital, pictures of his father as a young man, his grandfather, great-grandfather, and great-great-grandfather. He gave a rich and accurate portrait of Johnny Lanford. In fact, the only error in all his presentation hinged on the birth certificate that listed Jemima Lanford as his great-great-grandmother.

But that fact was a doozy, and I felt a little sheepish when I stood up and began my talk by simply refuting that one fact with evidence about Jemima Cavanaugh, wife of Johnny Lanford, and Jemima Lanford, wife of Franklin Margen. I shared the medical records and death certificate for Jemima Cavanaugh as well as the same image of the birth record Josh had shared about Jemima Lanford's delivery of Johnny. Then, I pointed out how Jemima Cavanaugh had already had a hysterectomy more than two decades before Jemima Lanford gave birth.

It was the same information we'd given Josh a few days prior, but this time when I looked at his face, I could see that the facts had sunk in. Maybe it was something about hearing it a second time or maybe the public forum, but Josh Lanford looked ashen and defeated. I felt terrible, but I had also hoped that this kind of understanding might come.

I spent a few minutes talking about Millie and Jemima Cavanaugh and gave Johnny Lanford the first his due, explaining how they had created their network designed to help women escape in a time when escape almost always seemed impossible. Then, I explained who Jemima Lanford (Jemima the Second) was and told the story of her abusive marriage, of how she had reached out to Millie through Johnny and gotten herself and her unborn son to safety. "These are some of the bravest people I have ever had the honor of studying, all three of them, and being a descendant of any one of them would be something I consider a great honor."

Mickey beamed at me from her seat, and while I couldn't get a read on her dad, a little of the color had come back into Josh's face.

So I moved to the second part of my presentation, which focused on the value of oral histories and family legends. I talked about how these family stories told important things about a family, about what they valued and what traits they appreciated in their ancestral lines. Then, I explained how much I could see of Johnny Lanford's good spirit and courageousness in the woman who had taken his name after she fled.

She needed to craft a new identity, I said, and she took the names of the two people who had saved her, Jemima and Lanford. "She did them a great honor by carrying their names forward, an honor that led us to know her descendants today." I pointed to the Lanford family, and when I looked carefully, I could see a tear on Josh's cheek. *The truth shall set you free*, I thought.

As I finished out my presentation with a round of thanks to everyone, including the Lanfords, who had helped with the research, Santiago stood and asked if he could have a minute of the group's attention.

I studied him a minute and when he didn't give me an indication of what he was going to say, I went ahead and took my seat to listen with everyone else. But when he began, I wasn't prepared for what he said, not at all.

"Ladies and gentlemen, as we've all learned tonight, history has a lot of twists and turns, and tonight, I find I need to tell you about another of the great mysteries here in Octonia. Last week, in the midst of a routine demolition of an outbuilding on a farm, the bones of a young man were discovered."

He allowed the shock of his announcement to pass through the room for a moment. Then he continued, "It has taken us a great deal of time to figure out who this man was, but I can tell you tonight, based on DNA evidence, that the man was Johnny Lanford, husband of Jemima Cavanaugh."

I felt my stomach plummet to my feet as I stared at my fiancé, who was now meeting my gaze with firm compassion. I quickly turned to Alexandra, who was also turned in her seat to look at me. She nodded to confirm what Santi had said.

"We do not know, at this time, the circumstances of Mr. Lanford's death, but I want to assure everyone here that we are doing everything we can to solve this mystery and provide Mr. Lanford and all of his family" – he looked from Jonathan to Josh then – "some answers. If you have any information that might be relevant, anything at all, please let me know. Thank you."

With that final word, he walked over and sat next to me. I found I couldn't stop staring at where he had been standing, even as people began to mill around. Finally, Santiago said, "Pais, I'm sorry I couldn't tell you. I didn't want that information to affect how you handled your presentation tonight."

I finally turned to look at him. "How long have you known?"

He sighed. "The DNA results just came back late this afternoon. I wasn't even sure I wanted to say anything, but when you handled this presentation with such grace and compassion tonight, I felt like it was the right forum to share that news." He took my hand. "I'm sorry I couldn't tell you in advance."

I could feel the anger inside my chest, but I knew that now wasn't the time to vent it. I also knew that my anger wasn't really justified. So I tamped it down, kissed Santi's hand, and went to talk with everyone.

Only an hour later, when everyone had left and I'd finally gotten a glass of white wine, did I pin down the question that had been teasing at the edge of my mind. Santiago was sitting in a chair across from me with Mika, Mary, and Alexandra on folding chairs around us in the Cozy Nook. "Whose DNA did you test?" I said without a preamble.

Everyone looked at me. "What?" Mika said.

"Whose DNA did you use to prove it was Johnny Lanford?" I said.

"Oh, Jonathan Boykins. He came in and gave a sample yesterday," Santiago said casually.

"Yesterday," I said. "You've suspected the person buried under Jackie's coop was Johnny Lanford for two days, long enough to have his descendant provide DNA, and yet you blindsided me with this information in a public forum tonight." It wasn't lost on me that I was doing a similar thing to him at that very moment, but I didn't care. "Wow," I said as I stood up, downed the few remaining sips of my wine, and picked up my bag.

I didn't look at anyone as I grabbed the tote with my projector and went out the front door. I was so angry that I knew I couldn't speak calmly. It was better that I just extricate myself from the situation.

I was halfway down the block to my car when I heard footsteps coming up quickly behind me. I spun around to tell Santiago I needed a little space when something heavy hit me in the temple and knocked me unconscious.

12

When I woke up, I was tied to a chair in what looked like every serial killer's basement I had ever seen on TV. The room was musty and dark, and only a single bare bulb provided light from a dozen feet away near a rickety wood staircase. I had the urge to scream, but I knew from instinct that the only person who would hear me was the one who had kidnapped me. Somehow, it seemed better to let that person think I was still unconscious.

I tried to free my hands and feet, but they were bound tight with what felt like shoelaces. I could see a greenish desk with a metal top against a wall just to my right, and in front of me on a small, black table I saw a bottle of Gatorade and a Luna bar. Despite my terror, I registered two things that made me laugh. First, that lemon-flavored Luna bar was my favorite. Second, I hated blue Gatorade. "One for two ain't bad," I whispered to myself.

As I sat there playing through every kidnapping scene I'd read or watched in my life, I contemplated choices from trying to break the chair to pieces – an idea I quickly discarded when I realized the chair was metal – to trying to hop myself up the stairs with the chair intact, another idea I tossed since I realized not breaking my neck was probably a good idea. I tried to shift my weight around to see if my phone was in my back pocket, but my bottom was too numb to tell. Besides, I told myself, any kidnapper with a brain would have taken my phone away.

Still, I couldn't fathom just sitting here and waiting for whoever this person was to come back. I wasn't good at simply sitting and waiting anytime, but especially not now. So I decided to hop around and see what I could see.

Of course, hopping while tied to a chair was easier said than done. Eventually I managed to get over to the table with the food and drink. Big lot of good that did me, of course, since I couldn't open anything. I thought about grabbing the bar with my teeth and dropping it into my lap to see if I could hold it still and bite it open. I decided against that for the moment though since it seemed a waste of time when I wasn't really hungry yet. Plus, the thought of poison wasn't far from my mind.

I looked around the room, hoping to see a mislaid knife or utility blade. Of course, I wasn't so lucky to have been kidnapped by someone with a lackadaisical attitude toward sharp objects. When this search didn't bring forth anything useful, I hopped my way toward the desk and as I got closer, I saw that there was a drawer in its side.

It took me another five minutes to get the final few feet, but when I did I contorted my body into a curve that let me grab the thin metal handle on the drawer with my teeth. It made a horrible screeching sound as I opened it, and I paused a moment, hoping that the high-pitched sound hadn't carried any more than my fumbling hops had.

When I didn't hear any sound of movement above me, I used my chin to pry the drawer open all the way even as I swore to myself and committed to a new neck workout as soon as I was free. The way my muscles were cramping spoke a lot to how much time I spent on the computer.

For the most part, the drawer was empty, but I did see a small slip of paper wedged under the edge of the left side. I tried to slide it free with my tongue, an action which resulted in me inhaling dust that was musty enough to have been from the nineteenth century. I leaned close and angled my head in such a way that I wasn't shading out the lightbulb's beam from above me.

The script on what appeared to be a small card was faint, like it had faded over time, but as I tilted my head further to get a better view, I could just make out the words *Registration Card* in red ink at the top. Beneath, I squinted to be able to read the name there: *Jonathan Lanford*.

I sat back so hard I nearly flipped myself over in the chair. I'd seen enough of those cards in my work to know that was a World War I draft registration card, and it had Johnny Lanford's name on it. What I couldn't figure out was why it was here.

Or more precisely, I couldn't figure out where I was.

I leaned closer to read the rest of the card, and I could see his address as Rural Route 3, which was the historical designation for the road I lived on, and his next of kin was listed as Jemima Cavanaugh at the same address. His occupation was given as "tanner," and the old tanyard up in town was listed as his employer. There was no doubt. This was Johnny Lanford's World War I card.

My fingers ached both from the tight bindings around my wrist and from the desire to look into the historical military records and see what I could find about Johnny's service, but for obvious reasons, research wasn't possible at the moment.

Instead, I thought back to information Josh Lanford had presented about Johnny. Nowhere in that talk had he said anything about Johnny serving in the military, and for anyone, that service was a big deal. But for the Lanfords especially, who had created a heroic image for their supposed ancestor, I couldn't imagine they would leave that out.

Plus, none of our research indicated anything at all about Johnny Lanford living anywhere here in Octonia. There was no hint he had traveled or left at any time. No, this draft card was just an odd thing given what I knew about Johnny.

But it did make me wonder where I was exactly. I wasn't sure, but I thought the address on the draft card might correspond to Jackie's house. Jackie's house didn't have a basement though, at least not one that I knew of. I supposed it was possible she did have a cellar, but she would have no use of it. But this space felt more raw than anything that would be under an occupied home. It felt like the air in here hadn't moved much at all in a very long time.

The muscles in my shoulders were really beginning to ache, so I decided to try to move around a bit more and see what else might be hidden in the shadows around me. The part of me that had read too many murder mysteries and seen far too many horror movies cautioned the other part of me that perhaps it was best to stay in the light, but caution wasn't really part of my usual MO.

So I decided to be strategic and begin near the stairs and then proceed around all the walls. At the very least, the action would keep me busy and occupied for a while so that the fear I could sense creeping up my spine might be kept at bay.

As I started up the first of the longer sides of the basement, I thought of the way Mom and I had always approached shopping at craft shows or street fairs – up one side and down the other. That way, we didn't miss a thing, and kept ourselves on the task at hand, which was, of course, seeing everything.

Halfway up the first wall, I noticed a series of holes drilled into the cinder block. They were about the same level as my head, which meant they hung about shoulder height for most people. I kept shuffling my way along the wall and pondered the regular intervals of the holes.

At first, I thought they had maybe held shelf brackets, but

they were too far apart for that. Then, I pondered if they might have been used to hang up tools. That didn't make sense either, though, because who spaced their tools out around the room? It just wasn't efficient. I kept eyeing the holes as I came to the first corner of my four-corner tour and decided they most have been used to mount a peg board like my dad had in his workshop.

Above me, I noted the nice-sized window, as far as basement windows go, that must have been placed there for ventilation or light. I couldn't get close enough to the height of the window to see if it was dark because of grime or because it was night outside.

I inched along beneath the window and had almost made it to the next corner when I saw something sticking out of one of the holes in the wall. I picked up my pace, even though my whole body ached from the way I had to basically fling my body forward with each movement, and when I got to the projectile, I almost shouted with glee. It was a rusty screw. Even better, it was a loose rusty screw – at least it looked loose in the shadow on the dark side of the basement.

I knew I had to get it out of the wall, but the problem was that I couldn't fathom how to reach the thing since it sat level with my hairline. I contemplated bouncing up and down until I hit it with my head, but since I wasn't sure the thing was going to simply fall from the masonry wall with a tap, I thought it better I not impale myself and, potentially, bleed to death in a basement where no one would ever find my body.

With a glance at the Gatorade bottle, I contemplated making my way to the bottle and somehow grabbing it behind my back before going back to the screw and chucking the bottle up into it. The problem was that if I missed with that one throw, I didn't think I would get another. The bottle would land on the ground, and I knew if I turned this chair over I wouldn't be able to get up, not as tired and sore as I was.

So, in the end, I opted to use two of my most ridiculous but frequently employed tools. The Stretch was from my work in architectural salvage. Saul made fun of me quite often for being too lazy or too impatient to go out and get a ladder. He'd come in, and there I'd be on the tippiest part of my tiptoes, reaching with a screwdriver to loosen the last screw in a corbel that I could have had down ten minutes earlier if I had just gotten the ladder.

The Tooth Grab was something I had perfected as a mother whose hands were always full with a pair of shoes, one sock, a drink, a snack, and some precious stick or slug that my son had found and wouldn't let me put down. Early on in motherhood, I had learned to carry the thing I needed most urgently to keep clean in my mouth. Typically, this was my own car keys or perhaps my own drink, but sometimes, I'd opted for shoes as the privileged items.

Now, I was hoping my stretching and tooth-grabbing skills were up for the task as I took a deep breath, focused on the way my mom would have been making me laugh with witty commentary about the art if we had, actually, been at a craft fair, and pushed myself and the chair up as high as I could manage.

Then, I jutted my chin up, wrapped my front teeth around that screw and jiggled for all I was worth. It hurt like hell, and I wasn't sure either my legs or my teeth were going to last long enough to get the thing loose. But just as I felt myself begin to tip over from fatigue, the screw popped loose from the wall, and I fell over backward with so much force that I felt my bones rattle.

But when the shock of the fall wore off, I had somehow managed to not only keep the screw in my teeth but also kept from swallowing it and choking on the tool of my salvation. I felt like a superhero.

My work wasn't done, though, because now I had to get the

screw from my mouth to my hands. Not at one moment of my life had I ever been coordinated enough to even imagine I could toss the thing over my head and catch it. So I opted for my usual physical prowess – dropping things.

I let the screw fall out of my mouth, and then I pushed the chair and myself onto our sides long enough to hear the screw fall to the concrete floor. At that point, I rolled myself onto my back and began scooting toward where I thought the screw had fallen.

For a few very painful and frustrating moments, I thought this was going to be like one of those times when Sawyer lost his pacifier during a tantrum and it rolled, by the power of a gremlin or some other evil magical being, into a corner of the house that disappeared every time I tried to look at it. But fortunately, it only took me a minute or two to feel the scrape of metal against my knuckle.

Then, I grabbed that beauty of a piece of metal and began to wear any remaining cartilage out of my hands by rubbing the threads of that screw against the black laces that held my hands taught.

Approximately eighteen hours later ... or maybe it was a brief few moments, I felt one of the pieces of string break, and when I wiggled my wrists, they came completely free. They had indeed been shoelaces, black in color, and apparently they had been tied with one very long and elaborate knot. As soon as they were loose, the blood rushed back to my hands, giving me the worst case of pins and needles I'd ever had.

As soon as I could move my fingers fully again, I flipped upright and pushed myself to standing before I bent over and took the screw to the strings around each of my ankles. A few minutes later I was free of the chair, rolling my ankles and pondering just how I was going to get out of that basement.

I had no idea what time it was, and I had no idea what waited for me upstairs. So I decided to try the window. It looked like it was big enough for me to squeeze through, and I hoped it would lead to the outside world and give me a chance to escape before whoever had locked me up even knew I was gone.

Fortunately, the little table with the Luna bar and the Gatorade was very sturdy, so when I carried it over and set it below the window, it held my weight. I studied the latch at the bottom of the window and quickly saw it swung up to open. Unfortunately, the simple mechanism that locked the window looked to be about a hundred years into epic rust production. I gave it a good push, but it didn't budge.

I climbed down off the table and studied my options. I could break the window, but that would definitely be loud and distinctive. I could try banging on the latch with, well, something, but again, a hammering sound of any sort might give me away. I scanned the room for anything that might help me pry the latch open.

That's when my eyes landed on the Gatorade again, and I gave thanks to God for social media because just a couple weeks before, I had gone down the rabbit hole of random links to watch a whole series of videos about how various beverages could dissolve rust. Beverages including Gatorade.

At that moment, I couldn't remember what it was in the beverages that did the trick, but I didn't care. I grabbed that blessed blue liquid and climbed back up on the table. Then, I ripped a strip from the bottom of my shirt, soaked it in Gatorade, and draped it around the latch.

In the videos, the experimenters had let the rusty objects soak for hours or even days, but I didn't have that kind of time. I had no idea when my kidnapper would come back, and I couldn't sit here and wait for science to do its slow but steady work. So I poured the rest of the drink over the piece of cloth, and then I started to wiggle the round latch back and forth as quietly but firmly as I could.

In just a few jiggles, the latch broke free. I pledged my loyalty to Gatorade forever and hoisted myself up and out of the window with the kind of strength I thought I'd only use if Sawyer were stuck under a car.

As I climbed up and out of the window well, I tried to get my bearings. It was very dark, so I hoped that meant I'd only been in there for a few hours. I didn't see any streetlights or road traffic, but that wasn't unusual in Octonia, especially late on a weeknight. But I could see a security light on the front of a barn that looked to be a far enough distance away to belong to someone other than the person who owned this house.

I didn't take much time to look carefully at the house I had been held captive in, partially because I didn't want to dawdle and partially because now that I was free, the idea of the place terrified me. But I did look back once and saw a nondescript white farmhouse, probably built in the 1950s, and a black pickup truck in the driveway. Then, I ran like hell.

The barn was across a narrow road that looked somewhat familiar but not familiar enough for me to really know where I was. Fortunately, a house sat just up the road from the barn, and when I knocked on the door, a man in boxers and a white T-shirt answered. I decided to overlook the shotgun in his hand and simply explained that I needed help and hoped I could use his phone.

He studied me for a minute, then looked behind him to a set of stairs. "Wanda, it's Lee Sutton's girl. Get the first aid kit and my phone." Then he led me to a Formica dining room table, poured me a glass of water, and let me call my daddy and my fiancé.

13

I woke up the next morning in my own bed with a little boy curled tight against my side. My entire body groaned when I moved even a finger, but I wasn't eager to move anyway. I was home and safe with my son. That was all I needed.

As I lay there, drifting in and out of sleep, I heard the distinct noises of cooking coming from downstairs. Soon, I smelled two of my favorite scents – coffee and bacon. About that same time, Sawyer snuggled closer against me and slid his head up onto my chest. "I missed you, Mama," he said.

I pulled him close and said, "I missed you, too, Saw. What happened while I was gone?"

He sat up and smiled. "I got to stay awake a long, long, long, long, long, long time." Then he frowned. "We didn't know where you were."

I levered myself up to sitting and drew him to me again. "I know, Love Bug. I'm sorry. Was that scary?"

He nodded.

I sighed. "I was scared, too, but I'm home ... and I smell bacon."

"Bacon!" Saw was up and out the bed before I could even tilt my legs toward the floor.

As he thundered down the stairs, I managed to get myself to a standing position and gave thanks that someone had dressed me in yoga pants and a T-shirt when they helped me into bed. Now, I didn't think I could possibly lift my arms or legs enough to put on clothes.

Slowly, I made my way downstairs, stifling a series of groans with each step, and settled myself quietly on the couch. From the kitchen, I could hear the voices of all the people I loved most: Sawyer, Santi, Dad, Lucille, and Mika, but I just needed another minute before I could face what would inevitably be a storm of questions.

Beauregard climbed up on my lap, and in a surprising moment of awareness and compassion, he refrained from his usual five-minute twist-and-turn routine to find the perfect spot. Instead, he purred against my fingers and laid down in a circle with his head on my hand. His gentle rumbling against my legs helped ease the discomfort just the littlest bit.

A few moments later, Saw came charging through the living room on his balance bike, and when he spotted me, he shouted, "Watch how fast I am, Mama," and proceeded to zoom past me into the hallway and back.

Since my presence had been sounded, I took a deep breath and watched for the concern that was about to pile through the kitchen door. But instead of four faces, just Santi came in, a cup of coffee in hand. He sat down next to me and handed me the mug. "How are you?" he said with such gentleness that I almost cried.

"Sore. Exhausted. But grateful." After I'd called Santi and then Dad, everyone, including Saw, had arrived at the farmhouse to get me. The farmers had been gracious hosts as Santi and Savannah had strategized their next moves. One option had been to raid the farmhouse where I'd been held right away.

Dad had been a big proponent of that course of action, but the police officers had decided against that choice. Their thought was that if, by chance, my kidnapper hadn't yet noticed my absence they might still have the element of surprise if they identified them before they struck. Besides, the truck that had been parked outside was gone, so the odds that the kidnapper wasn't there were high.

The conversation had gone on for a long time, but I fell asleep at some point as the exhaustion was catching up now that the adrenaline was gone. I had only flickering memories of getting into Santi's car and driving home. The last thing I remembered from the night was falling into bed with Sawyer.

"Did you do anything yet?" I asked as I sipped my coffee.

Santi shook his head. "Brett is staking out the house from the Grant place, and Savannah is on duty just up the road to keep an eye out for a truck like the one you saw heading this way."

I sighed. "Wait and see." It was a good choice, I knew, but it also made me uneasy. I was glad everyone was here to keep me company. To keep me safe.

"We made breakfast if you feel like eating," Santi said as I leaned my head on his shoulder. "Mika cooked up some French toast that she mentioned was your favorite."

My stomach growled, and I realized that I hadn't had anything to eat since lunch yesterday. That understanding brought back the way I'd stormed off in a temper tantrum because I'd felt excluded from something that wasn't really my place to be included in. "I'm sorry," I said.

"*You* have nothing to apologize for," Santi said.

I sat up and shook my head. "No, I do. I shouldn't have been so upset that you did your job without discussing it with me. I was being petty."

Santi pulled me against him again. "This case is important to you. I'm sorry I couldn't tell you."

"Now, *you* have nothing to apologize for." I sighed. "I don't remember much of last night. Did you find out who is renting the house?"

"Not yet," Santi said as he helped me to my feet. "The Grants, the couple who let you in last night, said that the people who ran the farm died a few years back. Now, their children own the place but haven't done anything with it since their parents passed."

I frowned as I walked toward the kitchen. "So who was there?"

"They didn't know. They thought maybe the children had rented out the place, but when I called the son this morning, he didn't know anything about someone living there." Santi paused as we passed through the kitchen door.

I looked at him. "So I went by today and found some old mail on the counter. Looks like Boykins might have been squatting there."

Mika, Dad, and Lucille all stopped in their silent movements around the kitchen and looked at me. Dad came over and gave me a quick hug, and then said, "Let's get this food on the table while it's hot."

I appreciated the care and the space, and since I had no idea what to do with the idea that Jonathan Boykins might have kidnapped me, I decided to just pretend I didn't know it. I took a seat at my table, trying not to wince too much when Sawyer climbed into my lap. Lucille set a plate of French toast and bacon in front of me, and then Mika slid a glass of orange juice over at the top of my plate. I wasn't going to be able to eat for a moment, until the little guy on my lap decided to move, but I was relishing his weight, even on my bruises, too much to move him yet.

"So someone has been squatting at that farm?" I asked as Sawyer leaned his cheek against my sternum and helped himself to a piece of my bacon.

"Sounds like it," Santi said.

"Did you see anything?" Mika asked as she sat down across from me.

I knew what she was asking. She wanted to know if I had seen anything about my attacker, but her question jogged loose a memory of the old green desk. "I did," I said with a lot more energy than anything else I'd said so far.

Everyone leaned forward, eager to hear, I expect, about the person who had kidnapped me, but instead, I said, "Johnny Lanford's draft card."

Lucille sat back and said, "What shot who?"

"Sorry," I said shaking my head a little. "In the basement where I was tied up. I found Johnny Lanford's draft card in the drawer of a desk."

Mika studied my face a minute and then said, "Why would his draft card have been there? That's too much to be a coincidence."

Lucille nodded. "So the person who you encountered last night has something to do with what you've been researching." She sighed. "We might have guessed that, I suppose."

Dad shook his head. "Why would we have made that connection? Paisley, for once, has been doing just what she was supposed to do."

"True," Santi said, "but maybe somebody thought she was getting too close."

"Too close to what?" Mika asked with anger. "This person died more than a hundred years ago. There's no way whoever did this is still alive. Who would care?"

I looked at her a long moment. "The same people who came to the presentation last night," I said as I felt a slow spread of understanding. "Everyone who came last night has a vested interest in the story of that person because they are his descendant, thought they were, or have owned the property the bones were found on."

Lucille sighed. "That's a lot of suspects," she said.

Dad was already on his feet. "Better get started rounding them up, Sheriff. That's a lot of questioning. Need some help?"

Santi shook his head. "Thanks, Lee, but we aren't going to just bring everyone in."

"Why not? Any one of those people might have been threatened by what Paisley found!" Dad was pacing now.

"Well, not all of them, Dad," I said, feeling my exhaustion reach a new level now that I had to talk my dad out of leading a real-life posse. "The coroner didn't kidnap me, and neither did our neighbor Jackie."

"You were kit-napped?" Sawyer said. "Wow."

I winced at his words. I hadn't been thinking when I said the word, but now I realized that everyone else had been talking in a sort of code to avoid scaring Sawyer. "Sorry, Love Bug. I'm totally okay now, but this is a conversation for grown-ups. What if Auntie Mika makes you a plate full of bacon and French toast with lots of syrup and you eat it in the living room with a movie?"

"I can eat in the living room?" he asked with eyes as big as eggs.

"Just this special time," I said and smiled at him. "But first give me a big hug."

He laughed, and while I suspected that the word *kidnapped* would stick in his brain and come back for conversation later, he didn't seem disturbed at the moment. He followed Mika to the stove and instructed her to give him five pieces of bacon, a request she gladly obliged at my nod.

With Sawyer safely ensconced in his favorite Lassie cartoon, I returned to our topic of conversation. "Dad, please sit down. It won't do us any good to alert the whole county about what happened, and that's exactly what will happen if we go hauling a bunch of people in."

I glanced over at Santiago, who was refilling coffee mugs,

and saw him nodding slightly. He would have told my dad that, if necessary, but I knew it was much easier for me to help calm my dad down, even if it was the last thing I wanted to do this morning.

"You were saying that it couldn't be Alexandra or Jackie," Lucille said, returning us to my earlier conversation. "Why is that?

"Well, first of all, Alexandra is an officer of the law. I know that doesn't rule her out entirely" – I sighed – "but she's also too short. Same goes for Jackie. The person who hit me was taller than me, not shorter."

Santi sat down and took out his notebook. "A lot taller?" he said with a raised eyebrow.

I thought back to the moment I felt something hit me in the head. The blow had come just as I turned around, and for a split second before the blow struck, I'd seen something that looked like a large-headed mallet coming down toward my head. "No, not a lot. Just enough that they hit me here," I pointed to the very sore spot just above my hairline on the left side of my head.

My fiancé made another note. "Anything else?"

My head was really starting to hurt, but I wanted to help catch the person who had done this to me. So I closed my eyes and tried to do what my meditation practice had taught me about letting my subconscious do the work. I took a few deep breaths, and then I realized I knew one more thing. "The person smelled like something, something I know, but I can't put my finger on what it was." I shook my head slightly and then squeezed my eyes shut against the pain. "Sorry, I know that's not helpful," I said as I opened my eyes and reached for my coffee.

Santiago sat down, rubbed my arm, and set another piece of bacon on my plate. "You did well, Pais. Now eat some more bacon."

It was only then that I realized I'd consumed everything on my plate without a thought. "Thanks. Is there any more French toast?" I asked as I realized I was still hungry.

"Coming right up," Mika said as she opened my fridge and took out the eggs, milk, and bread.

As she cooked a second batch of goodness, I recounted everything I could remember about the night from the moment I woke up tied to the chair to what was in the room to what I heard when I was there. Since the house had been almost entirely silent, the room almost empty, and the night dark, I had very little to share, but it felt good to put together the story, kind of like I was freeing myself from it or something.

Soon, though, it became clear we needed to do something. We had to find who had kidnapped me, and we needed to figure out why.

But first, some logistics to manage. Fortunately, Lucille had already called Sawyer's school, she let me know, and they were expecting him late this morning because of a family emergency. "I'll take him there and offer to stay and volunteer, just to keep an eye out for shifty folks."

I smiled at the thought of my stepmother taking on someone who came for my son – but then, if someone was that ignorant, they deserved the wrath of Baba. At that moment, she was sharing a final piece of bacon and taking on the sometimes Olympic-level task of getting Sawyer to choose his clothes and pack his things for school. Again, I felt teary, this time from gratitude. I'd take that help any morning, but especially this morning.

With Sawyer's plans squared, Claire good to manage my shop, and Mrs. Stephenson happy to cover for Mika, we began a full-scale charge to find out what exactly in the world and history was going on. Dad was itching to do something, so Santi asked him if he could please talk to the Grants to find out more about the man they'd seen at the farm where I'd been held.

Then, Santi called Brett to give him the heads-up and ask him to treat my dad like another deputy, but one without a gun or any authority. I appreciated that description.

Then, Santi asked if Mika and I could rally our research team and invite them to the sheriff's office to see what our historical sleuthing might yield by way of new information, especially concerning the draft registration card I'd seen for Johnny Lanford. I didn't know that we'd be able to figure out anything new, but I also knew my friends would do anything for me, especially if I was in danger.

True to form, Ms. Nicholas, Tee, Mary, and even Alexandra were already at the sheriff's office when Santi, Mika, and I arrived about an hour later. Both Mika and Santi had insisted I take a long hot bath and get ready slowly, and I'd done my best to relax and allow my body the pace it needed. But I was more anxious than anyone, except maybe my dad, to figure out what exactly was going on and how it was related to Johnny Lanford.

As I had expected, Santi put all his resources to work trying to find the black truck I'd seen and to find out if anyone had noticed my kidnapping from the street. Unfortunately, my limited description of the truck and the knowledge that the person was "a little taller than me" and "smelled like something I recognized" wasn't really much to go on, but he did his best.

While the six of us set up research stations, I heard him calling every police department in the area to ask for their assistance in the search and the loan of officers if they had any to spare. He was up front about the fact that his fiancée had been kidnapped and that this was, therefore, a bit personal in nature, but I knew he would have done the same for any of his constituents.

As soon as we had our laptops open, Ms. Nicholas pulled up the military archive database and searched for Johnny Lanford's draft registration card. She discovered it wasn't there, so she began making calls, starting with one to a colleague at the National Archives, where the original documents were filed.

Tee began combing the church records again to see if she could find any mention at all of Johnny's military service. Meanwhile, Mika looked for information in the local newspaper about the same thing.

Within an hour, we came to the conclusion that, as best we or anyone at the National Archives could tell, Johnny Lanford had never served any branch of the US Military. Not as Johnny, not as John, Jon, Jonathan, or any other variation of his name either. Our best guess was that he had filled out the registration card but never actually registered.

That theory pretty well established as far as we were concerned, we proceeded to review all the records we could to see if Johnny would have been excluded for service for an ailment, a particular family hardship, or maybe even as a conscientious objector. But nothing we could find indicated he had any legal reason to not have been recruited into the army as a soldier during World War I. He was the right age. He was able-bodied. He was not a registered pacifist.

All this information left us with one solid hypothesis: Johnny Lanford had purposefully avoided enlistment. Having been involved with a previous project that involved someone who had avoided the draft, I knew how high emotions could run about this kind of situation, especially in a fairly patriotic county like Octonia, so I hoped with all my heart that we could uncover a really good reason that Johnny Lanford had not done what most people would consider his civic duty.

Mary set out to look once again at the public records to see if we could find anything we'd missed that would give us more clues about Johnny Lanford's reasons for staying home. Ms. Nicholas delved into all the online medical record stashes she knew of and asked the volunteer on duty at the historical society museum to look through the local medical archives they had there.

Since Tee had brought along all the information she'd accrued about the Cavanaugh women and the Lanfords as well as a couple of miscellaneous boxes of files she had not yet sorted for the church, she and Mika dove right into the papers. And Alex jumped in to help Savannah and Santi by combing motor vehicle records since she had law enforcement experience.

I had my computer open but found I was too drained to make much sense of what I was seeing on the screen. So I did what I thought might actually be useful and pulled up a solitaire game to keep my "front of mind" busy while my "back of mind" turned over the questions we had behind the scenes. I figured if I couldn't be much good gathering new information, I might be able to connect some of what we already knew.

As each person found something they thought might be useful, they shared it with the room, and I listened carefully each time, then went back to my game. I was losing more than I was winning in solitaire, but even as tired as I was, I could feel the threads of a picture beginning to weave together in the back of my mind. The image wasn't clear yet, but it was forming.

For a couple of hours, all of us toiled away. Well, I clicked away and everyone else toiled, but I could feel the morale in the room starting to get low. The frustration in Santi's voice was becoming more apparent with every phone call he made, and I could hear the sighs from my friends as they worked around me.

Only Tee seemed still excited about her work, and I couldn't blame her. She was seeing old letters and documents for the first time since they'd been dropped into boxes and tucked into the storage room behind the pastor's office. As I tapped an ace of clubs over to its space on the screen, I listened to her delighted coos – and even occasional clapping – with satisfaction. She was feeling exactly the way I did when I went into an old building and started pulling off the crown molding. That old wallpaper back there, that was a story.

For a few minutes, I let myself quietly take joy in her discoveries, grateful this work had given her the chance to go through these boxes. Even if we couldn't find out who had kidnapped me or how that person was connected to Johnny Lanford, I was glad she'd been gifted a chance to do this work she so obviously loved.

I was just pondering what kind of wonderful binders she'd put together with her research when she slapped the table and said, "Shut the front door!" She looked up at me. "I found it, Paisley!"

All of us except Alex, who had taken a phone call, rushed over and stood around her as she pointed to an almost translucent piece of paper covered in the sepia-toned ink I knew so well. It was a letter, written by hand, and if I had to guess, the author was a woman. Even historically, men's script didn't usually have the loops and curls of women's handwriting.

"Listen, everyone," Tee said with the authority only a woman who almost single-handedly ran a church could have.

May 22, 1927

Dear Jemima,

We are well here in Charlottesville, and I must thank you and your beloved Johnny for that fact. Our residence is quite adequate, and I very much love our neighbors here in Vinegar Hill.

The women fawn over little John so much so that I think he will never want for babysitters. The men bring him sweets, and when he has enough teeth, they may simply fall out of his head.

I have long wanted to write and thank you, but as you know, I have much reason to fear discovery. But when I heard of your husband's passing, I could no longer justify my own silence.

I saw him recently, here in town, working under his own nom de plume at hotel on Main Street. I must say that his affected limp was quite convincing, and while we could not speak, we did exchange a gaze of recognition that seemed to speak all we needed to say to one another.

He was the best of men, Jemima. I know you know this to be true, and while you two had to hide much to stay in the service you had adopted as your own, I know that you chose such work, together and apart, out of love for all of us.

I pray that you will find peace in your loss and know that all of us whom you have served are grateful for your service, even if you cannot share the full nature of it as we wish you could.

With my deepest sympathies,
Jemima Lanford

P.S. It may give you some comfort to know that I have seen Mabel of late. Your Johnny, as his last act, was able to get her settled into a place of her own. She also sends her sympathy.

When Tee finished reading, I made my way back over to my seat and sat down heavily as I tried to let my brain weave this piece of information into the picture it had been pulling together. Johnny had died. He was working in Charlottesville. He had affected a limp. He was still helping women get settled there.

As if someone flashed a spotlight in my mind, I had it, and when I looked at my friends, I could see they were assembling the pieces, too. I sat forward and said, "Johnny stayed home to help Jemima help the women of Octonia, but to do it, he had to leave and go into hiding himself."

Tee nodded. "That's what I see in this letter, too, Paisley." She looked at the people standing near her. "Y'all think that."

Everyone nodded. "He was needed here more than he was there," Mika said softly.

"Talk about a hero," Ms. Nicholas added.

The depth of Johnny Lanford's sacrifice left us all a little speechless, and the silence sat in the air like gratitude for a long, long time.

Only the sound of Alexandra setting the desk phone back in its receiver lifted us out of our quiet stupor. She looked over at us. "What just happened?" she asked.

Tee told her about the letter, and Alexandra sighed. Then she stood up, walked over to where we were gathered and said, "Johnny Lanford died of leukemia."

14

All the quiet exhilaration that had filled the air around us a moment before deflated like a slashed tire. Cancer always did that, in my experience. It always took the best among us, including my mom, and it was indiscriminate. Despot, doctor, humanitarian aid worker, mother. It can come for anyone.

And it had come for Johnny Lanford.

After a minute, I forced myself to take a deep breath and said, "How did you find out?"

Alexandra sat down in a chair next to me, and the others around us followed suit. "I noticed anomalous spots on some of the bones, places that looked like the bone had swollen somehow. Those abnormalities got me thinking, so I sent some bones to the pathology lab. The science is still pretty new here, but their biopsies of the bones confirm this man died of leukemia."

I let my head fall back against the chair. "So he wasn't murdered."

She shook her head. "No, from the biopsy results, it seems

likely the cancer actually killed him. He was in the late stages of the disease."

"Why bury him the way they did?" Mary asked, forming the question that hadn't yet gotten to my lips.

Tee sighed. "Because she wanted him close, I expect. And probably didn't trust the yahoos around here to treat his grave with respect."

"But she buried him under her chicken coop!" Mika said.

I smiled. "He was close then, and if she's anything like me, she loved her chickens. Kept him safe all this time, too, didn't it?" I could see where Mika was coming from. Most people didn't like the idea of manure, but for those of us who were used to animals, it was simply part of life. In fact, I would have to ponder whether or not I wanted to be buried under the chicken coop myself.

Santi brought me back to reality, though, when he said, "But his body was disassembled. That's pretty morbid."

I had to admit I didn't have a ready answer for that, but Alexandra did. "Actually, it wasn't all that uncommon historically. People didn't use coffins for most of history, and a lot of culture lay bodies out to be taken back to the earth by her creatures. Maybe Jemima did the same."

"You mean she fed the vultures with him?" Mary said with a shake of her head. "Gives all kinds of new meaning to 'from the earth you came and to the earth you shall return.'"

A small smile played across Santi's lips, and when I saw it, I said, "What?"

"Maybe chicken poop wasn't so bad," he said.

It took a minute for the room to decide if that was too soon, but apparently, we didn't think so because a ripple of laughter passed around among us for a moment.

When the quiet settled back in, Ms. Nicholas said, "Let me see if I'm understanding our hypothesis here. To be able to keep helping women escape from abusive relationships, Johnny Lanford took a new identity in Charlottesville so that he could help the women Jemima sent him get settled. He took up a new name and even affected a limp."

"Maybe the limp wasn't affected?" Mika said.

"Maybe not," Alexandra said. "Either way, though, it helped him stay undetected."

Ms. Nicholas went on. "Then, when he died of leukemia" – she looked at me – "his wife Jemima brought him home, left his body out in the elements, and then buried his bones under her chicken coop." She raised one eyebrow. "That's a big story, Paisley Sutton."

"It is," I said, "and we're just stringing together a bunch of pieces to make a story. But it sounds like it all lines up to me." I sighed. "I would like to find out more about Johnny's death, though."

"I'll be damned," Tee whispered under her breath as I finished. "'Johnny T. Lanford was laid to his final resting place on this day in November, 1927.'" She pointed to a slim piece of paper about the size of a bookmark. "'In attendance were his wife, six women whose names will not be listed to protect their identities, and eight trusted men of the church. In accordance with his wishes, he was buried with his birds where his wife could talk to him every day.'"

I stood up and walked over to Tee. There, on the table before her, was the same kind of memorial card I had in my dad's childhood Bible to remember his father's funeral. But this one was handwritten, and on the reverse, someone had done a rough sketch of the chicken coop we had disassembled the week before.

"Whoa," I said, and reached back to catch myself, only to find Santi there, his firm chest holding me up.

"Time for you to get some rest. Any more mysteries can wait," he said as he led me back to my chair.

I nodded, too taken by all we'd found this morning and my exhaustion from the night before, to protest. Mika brought me a cup of hot tea, and everyone else began packing up our research tools. We'd found the answers we could, and now, it was time to tell the tale.

Or it would be, as soon as I could think clearly again. I put my head down on the table to rest and heard Santiago ask Tee if she could make copies of those documents for him and for me, a task she gladly agreed to do. He also asked everyone to keep what we'd discovered quiet until we could determine how all this related to my kidnapping.

I expect the conversation went on for a bit beyond that, but I fell asleep on my arm, just like I was back in third grade.

UNFORTUNATELY, I wasn't as limber as I had been in third grade, so when I woke up a bit later, my left shoulder throbbed from being wedged up higher than usual for longer than usual. The pins and needles washed down my arm like a waterfall of thorns, and I shook out my arm and looked around.

Everyone had gone, except Santiago, who was sitting at the table next to me, his notes spread in front of him. He was looking at me, and he looked worried. "I didn't want to wake you," he said and then looked at my arm as I rubbed circulation back into it. "Maybe I should have."

I shook my head. "No, that sleep was good ... and my arm will be fine. Figure anything new out?" I leaned over to glance at his notes.

He slid an arm around my waist and pulled my chair closer. "Unfortunately not. Everyone is looking, but a lot of people drive black pickups around here."

I sighed. "Yeah, I wish I'd gotten more information, but I'm not going to hold myself too accountable since I was running for my life and all."

Santi smiled. “Exactly. We’ll find who did this, Pais.” He planted a soft kiss on my temple. “But right now, I’m going to get you home, make you some soup, get out your stitching, and turn on your favorite show.”

I laid my head on his shoulder. “You’re too good to me,” I whispered.

“Impossible,” he said as he helped me to my feet.

An hour later, I was watching *The Book of Boba Fett*, eating tomato soup with cheddar cheese and saltines in it, and looking forward to getting some work in on the paisley pattern. My brain was still working overtime and trying to figure out who might have kidnapped me. I just couldn’t fathom what I had done to become a threat to anyone in my research, and that’s the only reason I could figure out why someone would want to hurt me.

Unless, of course, Josh Lanford had just been acting the night before and he was still holding a grudge because I’d told the truth about his family lineage. But I just didn’t think he had done this. It seemed like he, his sister, and their dad had all felt pretty good when they left last night. Mickey had even suggested we get a drink sometime, and I was looking forward to that girls’ night out.

But as I picked up my stitching, I was no closer to having a theory about who wanted to get me out of the picture, and I decided to give my brain a rest, disappear into whatever planet Boba Fett was on today, and try to be sure I wasn’t conflating Ming-Na Wen’s character with her equally tough one from *Agents of S.H.I.E.L.D.* I was going to have to let Santi and his makeshift sheriff’s office in the kitchen do the work.

When Sawyer came home from school a couple of hours later, he charged into the living room, looked over his shoulder, and then quietly walked the rest of the way over to me.

"Hi, Mama," he said and laid his head on my chest. "I love you."

"I love you, too, Saw, but what's this quiet ... it's tickle time," I said, scooping him up and tickling all his most vulnerable spots until he was breathless. It took most of the energy I had recouped over the afternoon to give him that piece of normalcy, but it was worth it because when he got up and went outside with his Boppy to start on his treehouse, he barely gave me another look.

Lucille sat down, picked up my feet, and began to rub them gently. I sighed and slid down against the arm of the couch. "Thank you," I said. "Everything go okay at school?"

"No problems at all. I love that place. They even had an off-duty police officer from Charlottesville come by and spend most of the day, just in case." She sighed. "I might just volunteer there more often. I kind of like playground duty."

"Sawyer would love that and so would the school, I bet. Thanks for being there. I felt better just knowing you were on site with him if anything should happen." I sighed. "Did you hear the news about Johnny Lanford?"

"Santi texted. Wow. That's all something. Staying home to help. Hiding. Dying. Spending eternity under chicken butts." She smiled. "That's a good man."

I laughed. "Agreed. I'm thinking I might forego a plot for Santiago and make similar arrangements for when he dies."

"Hardy har har," he said from the kitchen. "How do you feel about being placed inside a statue to honor you at the courthouse?"

"Will it replace the Confederate soldier there?" I asked.

"I can see what I can do," he said.

"If you can make that happen, I'm in." I laughed and pushed myself upright. "What can I make everyone for dinner?" I said as I stood up.

"Paisley Sutton, you sit back down," Lucille said with a

voice that was, I'm sure, very effective on playground duty. "I'm on my way to pick up burgers and fries for all of us downtown. You will not be doing any cooking for the rest of this week."

"Take Lee," Santi said as he passed her in the doorway. "Don't want any of you alone just now."

Lucille nodded and went out the back door to find her husband and grandson.

I looked at Santi. "You're that worried?"

"I am." He looked out the window where Sawyer was baiting his grandparents into a game of tag. "If I understood the why of the whole thing ..."

I leaned back against the couch and put my feet back on the ottoman. "I have a theory about that. What if someone didn't want me to figure out who was buried under the coop?"

"Why would that matter?" Santi asked as he sat back next to me. "The guy has been dead for almost a hundred years."

"You saw how Josh Lanford and his dad reacted about finding out that the man they revered wasn't their ancestor. What if someone was ashamed of the fact that he didn't go into the war? We've seen that before."

A puff of air spewed from Santiago's lips. "We have, and I guess that's a possibility. But it wouldn't have been Josh who kidnapped you, not after you clarified who his real ancestors were."

I nodded. "Right. At least I don't think so. He seemed pretty chilled out last night. So did his dad, and I don't think his dad could have gotten me into that basement and tied me up like that." The vision of the older man with the walker just didn't align with that theory.

"No, I don't think so either. But that's the problem. I don't have any suspects." He pulled his hand down his face and stretched his skin long over his cheekbones.

I leaned into him as I heard Dad's car start. When I walked

to the front door, Lucille met me and said, “Saw wants to go along. Do you mind?”

“Of course not,” I said and waved to where he was already climbing into the back seat of their car to have my dad strap him in. “Can I please give you some money?”

My stepmother looked at me, turned without a word, and walked down the sidewalk. I took that as a no.

I watched Dad back out past my car and waved to Sawyer as they went up the driveway. Then, I took a long, deep breath of the fall air and went back inside. The soup had been delicious, but it had also faded away. Those burgers sounded amazing, and I knew my stepmother: we’d have some bonus treats, too.

As I sat back down next to Santi and picked up my sewing, I pictured how good the deep-fried mushrooms were going to be. Santi lifted his arm as I swung my legs over his lap and leaned back. He had his phone in his other hand, and I could see he was reading some article, probably some landscaping article since he now had a whole new yard to play in.

A couple of minutes later, just as I was going back to a teal green thread I had parked a couple days back, I heard tires on the gravel outside. “They must have forgotten something,” I said as I stood up and walked back to the door, scanning the kitchen for my dad’s phone or wallet, the two objects he most often left behind.

Seeing neither, I stepped out onto the porch to ask if everything was okay and caught just a glimpse of a black pick-up before a hand clamped over my mouth from behind. A second later, a bag slipped down past my eyes, and I was in the dark. I tried to scream against the hand; tried to bite it, too, but the fingers were thick and calloused. No matter how hard I chomped down, that hand didn’t move.

When the person holding my head spun me around, my own hand brushed against another arm and I quickly realized there were two people. I was pushed inside my house, and the door slammed behind me. A man's voice just behind my head said, "Find some rope. Thick rope this time. I don't want her getting away again."

The other person moved to my right, toward the living room where Santiago was sitting. I tried to scream and warn him, but as I took a deep breath to scream, the hand clamped tighter against my lips and teeth. "Stay quiet," he said in my ear. "Don't need the neighbors getting worried."

I thought about Jackie, about Rick who lived on the other side of the stream. Sawyer screamed like a wild man most days, and none of my neighbors had ever mentioned it. We were just too isolated here. But if this person thought I could get help, that was only to my advantage. At least I hoped it was.

A couple moments later, I was forced down into what I recognized as one of my dining room chairs, and my hands and feet were bound just as they had been the night before, but tighter. The bruises on my wrists and ankles screamed as the ropes were pulled tight, but I refused to let these awful people know I was in pain.

"Could I have a glass of water?" I said instead of shouting. "You wouldn't believe the last twenty-four hours I've had, and I'm pretty dehydrated. Someone gave me a Gatorade last night, but I had to use it to free some rust instead of drink it. Go figure."

I knew I was egging them on, but they were in my house, for goodness' sake, and if they had come just a few minutes earlier, my child would have been here.

That thought brought me up short. They had waited until Dad, Lucille, and Saw left. They thought I was alone now. Santiago had driven my car back from town. They didn't know he was here. I steadied my breath. "Please. Seriously. I'm thirsty."

"Get her some water," the man said. Now that he was a bit

further away from me, I found his voice to be a little familiar, but I couldn't place it. Maybe because I was terrified. Again.

"Why are you doing this? What have I done?"

I heard someone walk toward my sink and turn on the faucet. Instinctively, I said, "The fridge water is better. Filtered again." I rolled my eyes at myself. Yes, please, let me worry about another level of filtering on my death water.

A second later, footfalls came back my way. "Here you go," a woman's voice said, and I heard the thunk of a glass on my table.

I reached forward and grabbed the glass, thinking that if one of them just spoke again I could fling the glass at them and make a break for the door. But no one spoke, and I quickly realized that I wasn't, even with sight, likely to get away. And blindfolded I'd be as likely to knock myself on the doorframe as make a run for it.

I sipped the water instead and held my breath as the heavier pair of footsteps walked away from me toward the living room. I hoped Santiago had made a break for it out the front door and was bringing backup as we spoke. I knew he wasn't still sitting on the couch reading his phone. But what I didn't know was where he was exactly.

"We're not waiting this time," the woman said. It sounded like she was facing away from me. "That was our mistake yesterday. We take care of this now."

I could only imagine "this" was me and that they weren't going to wait to kill me this time. But I was bound – pun intended – and determined to at least know why I was going to die if I was going to die.

"All right, then, at least tell me why you're doing this. I really can't figure it out." I let a little whine slip into my voice, a la Sawyer, and hoped that either the desperation or the annoying tone would stir them to start talking.

Someone sat down across from me, and I heard a heavy

sigh. "Those bones were meant to stay buried," she said. "Jemima wanted it that way, and then you go and tear them out of the ground like some sort of buried treasure. That ain't no way to treat the dead."

This woman's voice sounded familiar, too, but again, I found I couldn't attach an identity to the sound. "I didn't know that Jemima had put him there," I said trying to sound as sincere as I felt. "I went to take down a building, and we found a person buried there. I couldn't just leave the bones where they were. I thought someone had been murdered."

"No one was murdered," the man said as he returned from wherever he'd been. "Aunt Jemima did just as Johnny wished. You and your nosy self, just asking too many questions."

Aunt Jemima, I thought, and suddenly, I knew it was Jonathan Boykins there in the room with me. "I meant no disrespect," I said, deciding not to let my kidnappers know I recognized one of them. "Surely, you can understand this was all a good-hearted mistake." I was being generous to call what we'd done a *mistake*, but I was hoping generosity might save my life.

"And what was it when you broke my daddy's heart and told him his grandaddy wasn't a hero after all but some wife-beating monster?" the woman said.

It took me a minute to put together what she was saying, but then I realized I was talking to Mickey Lanford, Josh's sister who had played like she was so happy I was telling the truth. Fool me once ... and I'd been fooled twice in the last week by people who had pretended to be in support of what I was doing.

Figuring now that we all knew the jig was up, I said, "Jonathan, Mickey, you have to believe that I really was trying to do the right thing." I sighed. "Can you take this hood off me? I know who you are."

"Might as well," Jonathan said as he whipped the thing off

my head hard enough to send my chin flying into the air behind it. "You really do think you're so smart, don't you?"

I looked from him to her and was met with dead-eyed stares from both. "No, I don't. Not now that I realize how much I've hurt you. I thought I was helping, but obviously, some things are better left unknown." I had to really work to choke out those words because I had basically founded my life's work on the opposite philosophy, but it seemed like what they wanted to hear.

It also seemed like my efforts at appeasement were failing, if I could judge anything by the death stares I was getting. For a brief second I let my mind wander and pondered if I could pull off a Death Star/death stare joke, but I quickly decided against it because, well, death stares. Not death stars. Those would have been more fun, I think.

"What can I do? How can I fix this?" I said and felt a bit like one of those scuzzy businessmen in B-movies.

Mickey rolled her eyes. "There's no fixing this, Paisley. The harm has been done. We're just trying to keep you from doing more harm."

"What more harm could I do? People know your ancestor was buried under that coop, Jonathan. You helped Santiago figure that out." I remembered the look of satisfaction on Jonathan's face when Santiago had made his announcement the night before. "He said you volunteered it."

"Damage control," Jonathan said. "I figured if everyone knew who the body was you would leave it alone. But then after that presentation, I hear you telling those people who stole my family's name that you're still researching. We couldn't have that."

I sighed. There really were no secrets in a small town. "So you thought you could stop me before I got more research done." It wasn't a question.

"And we're going to," Mickey said. "That chicken coop out there looks light enough to lift, don't you think, Jonny?"

I looked at Jonathan Boykins. "You go by Jonny?"

"Always have. Just like my great-grandaddy. Got a problem with that?" He stepped closer, and for a split second I felt like I was about to get into one of those fights kids got into on the playground.

"Nope, no problem here," I said. "I just didn't know that."

"Because I didn't want that name on your lips," he said.

I clearly had misread him when we met last week. The venom and ire in his voice now were palpable.

"First that woman steals my family's house, and now you're trying to steal our reputation." He looked at me closely. "You're old Octonia, too, Paisley Sutton. Didn't your daddy teach you better?"

There are only a few things that can get me to lose my temper – one is threatening my son. The second is disparaging my daddy. "Listen, you," I said, trying to stand up and feeling the bruises on my ankles shout again. "My father raised me right. He taught me to respect the truth, all of it, even when we don't like it. He taught me not to keep secrets because it's in the secrets that the shadows decay. And he taught me to respect people I disagreed with."

At that moment, the window beside me crashed in, and Santiago knocked Mickey aside and tackled Jonathan. It was the most superhero move ever.

I rammed the chair back hard against the refrigerator and felt the spindles behind me, weakened by Saw's continual climbing on the furniture, break loose. I freed my hands and dragged the chair behind me before slamming it onto Mickey's chest as she tried to get up from the floor.

A moment later, Santiago handcuffed her to a leg of my heavy dining room table and then freed my ankles. At that point, I almost collapsed onto the floor, but Santiago helped me to another chair while he opened the door for Savannah, who was running full-tilt toward the house.

When she came in, she looked around and then said, "And you needed me because ...?"

I laughed. "Superman here took care of it all."

"Are you kidding?" he said. "That WWE move with the chair was classic."

Savannah looked from Santi to me and back to him. "You both need your heads checked after this stunt." She glanced over at the window. "You did not jump through a window, Sheriff."

"He most certainly did." I was grinning now, even as a deepening fatigue began to settle into my bones. "That was some move."

He sighed. "Your son taught me that."

"What?! Sawyer has never crashed through a window," I said.

"Yet," Savannah added.

"Yet," I agreed. "But what do you mean?"

"Oh, he showed me how to get on the roof from his bedroom window, then climb down to the creamery, where I could jump to the ground." He looked at me. "We've also discussed rappelling down and coming in the windows, but I couldn't find any rope that was strong enough to hold me."

I shook my head. "I knew he got onto the roof, but I had no idea he could get down." I sighed. "Please don't show him how to rappel, okay?"

"I make no promises," he said. Then he turned to Jonathan and Mickey. "You two ready for a cozy night?"

"We're not together," Mickey said with a sneer.

"Then why are you helping him?" I asked, realizing as I said it that I knew exactly why. "You felt the same way your dad and brother did." I had been so blind.

"Johnny Lanford is a hero. And you're out here telling secrets that aren't yours to tell." Mickey's voice was full of anger.

"For the record, we all know that Johnny avoided military service during World War I, and we all think he was a hero for it. I saw that you had his desk – it was his desk, right? – in the house where you've been sleeping. You kept it as a memento, something you could have to remember him because you admired him so much. He stayed behind to help his wife and the women of Octonia, and I think he's a hero, too." I sighed. "If you'd give people a chance with the truth, you might find out that most of us can appreciate the facts and the people who lived them just as much as we can any legends we find."

Mickey stared at me. "You know?"

"I'm not the only one," I said. "So you see, killing me would have been a real waste." I shuddered, but I was telling the truth. There was no way my friends would have failed Jemima and Johnny by keeping their story quiet.

"I do have one question, though," I said, turning to Jonathan. "I realize that Jemima was worried about Johnny's reputation if people found out he didn't serve, but did she ask her family to keep her secret, too? Was your mom told to keep this all in the family?"

Jonathan shook his head. "Nope, Mama tried to get me to talk about Johnny in a paper in fifth grade. She and Aunt Jemima were right proud of him. But this was family business. Nobody else needed to know."

I could have said about a hundred things in objection to that statement, but I'd learned long ago not to fight with people who have already decided something is true and irrefutable. Clearly, Jonathan was not going to be moved from his position about Johnny's story.

Fortunately, stories belong to all of us, within reason, of course, and I was eager to get this one out into the world. Once I recovered.

Savannah and Santi loaded the two kidnappers into her cruiser, and when Dad and Lucille returned at the same time, Santi decided to go into town to help his deputies with the paperwork. "You're safe now. Save my burger for me?"

"I make no promises," I said. "But given your entrance skills earlier, I think I can arrange that." I gave him a soft kiss and then followed the rest of my family inside.

15

I imagine there are some people who cannot eat after having been kidnapped, especially if they've been kidnapped twice. I am not one of those people. As soon as the cruiser left, I sent Sawyer to wash his hands so I could fill Dad and Lucille in, and then we sat down to eat. Santi was lucky I loved him because I really did eye up his burger pretty hard. But when Lucille produced sugar cookies with smiley faces from the stash of baked goods that I really was beginning to believe she kept in her car at all times, I settled for three of those. Then, the four of us settled in to watch *Encanto* while we waited for Santi to come home.

The next thing I knew, it was the middle of the night. Sawyer and I were curled up under a pile of blankets, and Santiago was asleep on the other wing of the L-shaped couch. I looked at my two boys sleeping soundly, both drooling like they had a pool to fill, and I smiled. For a split second, I thought about waking Santi and carrying Sawyer up to bed, but then I sighed and tucked myself back in between my son and my cat and went back to sleep.

. . .

When I woke up again, the sun was streaming in and I could smell coffee from the kitchen. Sawyer was awake and watching *Encanto* again, and when I ruffled his hair, he said, "Mama, will you take me to school today?"

"Of course, Love Bug." But first, I needed a shower and some of that coffee.

I made my way into the kitchen to find that delicious elixir and found Santiago, in full uniform, at the stove making oatmeal. "Good morning," I said as I slid my hands around his waist. "Thank you."

"For what?" he said as he kissed my cheek.

"For cuddling us up," I said.

"Oh, I didn't do that. You two were already out and cuddled when I got back." He stepped out of my arms toward the coffee pot. "I think your dad and stepmom needed to take care of you."

"Well, you slept on the couch, too," I said as I took the coffee.

"You think I was going to let you sleep on the couch and go take the comfy bed? You think I wanted to hear about the time I did that for the rest of my life?" He stepped toward me and pulled me against his chest as I swung the coffee wide. "I'm not a dumb man, Paisley Sutton."

"No, sir, no you are not." I gave him a quick kiss and then took my coffee into the bathroom with me. I couldn't stand to be far away from coffee today.

After dropping Sawyer at school, I went into Mika's shop after picking up lattes and chocolate croissants. Today, I was going to drink and eat whatever I wanted, and later I was going to take a long, hard nap. But first, I needed to see my best friend and figure out what we needed to do for Saturday's event. It was only two days away, and I knew there was lots to do.

Fortunately, Mary was already there when I arrived, and she had gladly taken on the role of organization for Women of the Skein, a role both Mika and I were glad to relinquish. It turned out that she and the women from church had personally visited all the yarn bombing sites in the past two days and were creating even more signage for each voting location as well as organizing a driving tour to get people to all the stops, and were working with Lucille for the cake walk and bake sale. Everything was well in hand.

"So what can I do to help?" I said, feeling a little left out.

"You have to do the main bit of publicity, Paisley," Mary said. "I need some content for the press release, so I need your follow-up article about Millie and Jemima. Johnny too. Can you get that to me tomorrow?"

I smiled. "I'll write it up today. It'll actually help me process through the past couple of days. Send it over via email?"

"Woman, I'm on your mailing list, so just send it out as usual. I'll get what I need and put this out first thing tomorrow." Mary waved a piece of paper in front of me like a flag. "Now, you go home and rest."

Mika smiled and took my arm as we walked to the door. "I'm glad you're okay, but please never send me another text that says, in full, 'I was kidnapped again.'"

In my haste to connect with the woman I loved more than any other in the world, I had sent that terrifying text, which had prompted her to call first me, then Santi, then Lucille until Lucille answered, told her I was fine and asleep on the couch, and that I'd see her tomorrow.

"I'm so sorry," I said. "I was a little out of it."

She hugged me and told me she was bringing dinner tonight. "Don't even try to refuse. Lucille is making it, and I'm just bringing it so I can eat some. She insisted."

I laughed. "All right, see you later. I better get home and write for Mary."

The article basically wrote itself. I began by recapping what I'd shared about Millie and Jemima the previous week, and then I talked about how Jemima had picked up her mother's legacy with her secret husband Johnny Lanford. I discussed Johnny's role of information courier and, later, concierge for the women of Octonia who moved to Charlottesville.

I ended the article by discussing how Johnny had sacrificed his chance to serve his country so that he could stay and serve his community. I lauded the personal choices that kept him safe from arrest and societal retribution – his secret marriage and his eventual move to Charlottesville under an assumed name. Finally, I talked about how his grieving wife had brought his body home and secreted it away so that he would remain close to her and so that his final resting place would be honored.

I then inserted a photo that Jackie had just sent me. It showed a small bronze plaque that now sat on an old millstone Jackie had erected near the former site of the chicken coop. The plaque read, *In Honor of Millie Cavanaugh, Jemima Cavanaugh, and Johnny Lanford, who saved countless lives and preserved happiness for so many people in Octonia and beyond.*

Jackie had commissioned the plaque as soon as she'd learned the story of the people who had owned her home, and after hearing about the article she'd wanted to speed along the small memorial she was going to give them. Today, when I'd asked for a photo, she had been happy to oblige, and while I had not yet told her about how Jonathan Boykins had resented her when he sold her his family homestead, I knew she would understand that, too. She was that kind of generous spirit.

But alas, the law was not of the forgiving kind, and Boykins and Lanford had both been arraigned this morning and charged with kidnapping and a host of other similar charges for their actions against me. Their trial would be in a few weeks, and Santi felt confident they'd both do time for their crimes.

In preparation for the arraignment, Santi and Savannah had pulled all the information they could about both Jonathan and Mickey, and Santi had let me know that Boykins had sold his family home because his cabinet shop had taken a major hit financially in the past few years as cheaper, pre-manufactured options for cabinets and furniture moved closer to Octonia. He'd had to sell, it seemed, to save his business.

I felt terrible that he had been in that situation. Even though my home wasn't one my family had owned for generations, I would still have felt profoundly sad to lose it, even if it was to save my business. Homes have spirits, and losing one of them can feel like losing a person you care about. That's part of why I worked so hard to keep some of these old places alive – their stories mattered.

But no amount of sadness and grief justified what Boykins and Lanford had done, and I felt confident that all of their ancestors would be glad to see justice served, especially since the system had failed so many of them in the past.

TWO DAYS PASSED IN A FLASH, and on Saturday afternoon, Sawyer and his dad and his dad's fiancée joined Santiago and me at Mika's store for the first stop on the Women of the Skein event. I was there mostly as a spectator, but I did have the opportunity to answer a few questions and direct people to the historical society building for a more in-depth talk about the Cavanaughs and the Lanfords.

Ms. Nicholas had jumped at the chance to both raise money for Warm Up America and do a little historical reenacting at the museum. Today, local folks were performing in period costume as Millie, Jemima, and Johnny, and the local news agencies had gobbled up the story for their early evening shows.

The yarn bombing was on in full force around Octonia, and as the five of us began the driving tour, Sawyer pointed out all the yarn that adorned his hometown. Children had yarn bombed road signs and lampposts, and most of the local businesses had also contributed some bit of decoration to the day.

But it was the big displays that really captured the imagination. At Sawyer's school, the teachers had created an entire Wonderland on the playground, complete with a yarn Cheshire cat and a tea party. And over at Bethel Church, the members had gone all out and yarn bombed their entire fellowship hall in yellow, green, and red yarn. But it was the sheriff's office that really won my heart. There, the three officers had turned a cruiser into a horse, complete with one hoof that stomped when it was activated by a voice command. If we had let him, Saw would have told the horse to stomp for hours.

We couldn't stay for hours, though, because I was part of the voting team to see who had won the competition, and Sawyer was going to draw the names for the door prizes.

When Sawyer's school won the competition, he cheered so loudly that several people in Mika's shop put their hands over their ears, but it was the way his teacher teared up when he gave her the gift certificate for "a lifetime's supply of yarn" that got to me. "We'll have craft supplies forever," she said.

Each of the winners of the various door prizes from the businesses around town was equally gracious to my son as he gave them their winnings. That extroverted boy of mine was in hog heaven with all the attention.

After everyone had left and Sawyer had gone home with his dad, we all – Mary, Santiago, Chris, Mika, and I – sat down for a beer and to relax a bit. Everyone was exhausted: Mika because of the monumental work she had put into the event, the guys from supporting the women they loved in every way, and me from two kidnappings in two days. We could all have gone straight to bed, but a day like this called for a good wind-down with good friends.

"So how did you think it went?" I asked Mika after taking a long pull from my beer. "Were you pleased?"

Mika nodded. "Very. I loved how many people participated, and I really loved the way the historical society took on the stories and made them literally come alive. And I'm really glad the school won the competition." She glanced over at Santi. "No offense."

"None taken. What would we have done with a lifetime supply of yarn?" he said with a wink. "But was it enough, Mika?"

She looked at Chris and then at me. "It was. I gave my landlord the check and signed the deed this afternoon. The building is officially mine."

I clapped my hands, and Chris gave Mika a long kiss before producing a bottle of champagne and popping the cork all the way across the store. "This calls for a celebration," he said.

"Yes, yes, it does," I said as I got up, grabbed champagne glasses and handed them out as Chris filled them.

"A toast?" Mary asked.

"A toast: to women and all those who love them. May we be them. May we raise them," Mika said.

"I can drink to that," I said. "I can drink to that."

Read the next of Paisley's adventures in *Strangled Skein* - https://books2read.com/strangledskein.

A FREE COZY SET IN SAN FRANCISCO

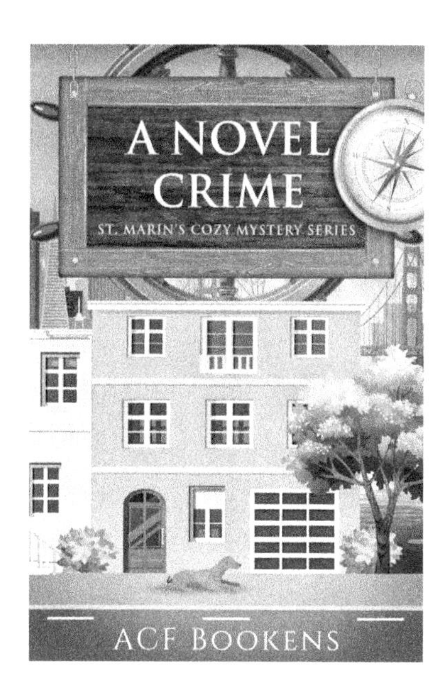

Join my Cozy Up email group for weekly book recommendations & a FREE copy of *A Novel Crime*, the prequel to my St. Marin's Cozy Mystery Series.

Sign-up here - https://bookens.andilit.com/CozyUp

ALSO BY ACF BOOKENS

St. Marin's Cozy Mystery Series

Publishable By Death

Entitled To Kill

Bound To Execute

Plotted For Murder

Tome To Tomb

Scripted To Slay

Proof Of Death

Epilogue of An Epitaph

Hardcover Homicide

Picture Book Peril

Stitches In Crime Series

Crossed By Death

Bobbins and Bodies

Hanged By A Thread

Counted Corpse

Stitch X For Murder

Sewn At The Crime

Blood And Backstitches

Fatal Floss

Strangled Skein

Aida Time

Poe Baxter Books Series

Fatalities And Folios

Massacre And Margins

Butchery And Bindings

Monograph and Murder - Coming in February 2023

Spines and Slaughter - Coming in March 2023

ABOUT THE AUTHOR

ACF Bookens lives in Virginia's Southwestern Mountains with her young son, old hound, and a bully mix who has already eaten two couches. When she's not writing, she cross-stitches, watches YA fantasy shows, and grows massive quantities of cucumbers. Find her at acfbookens.com.

Printed in the USA
CPSIA information can be obtained
at www.ICGtesting.com
LVHW022156141024
793833LV00024B/597